Shyt List 6: The Original Bitch Of Revenge Returns   **1**
Returns

SHYT LIST VI

THE ORIGINAL BITCH OF REVENGE RETURNS

a novel by Reign

By Reign

ARE YOU ON OUR EMAIL LIST?
SIGN UP ON OUR WEBSITE
www.thecartelpublications.com
OR TEXT THE WORD:
CARTELBOOKS TO 22828
FOR PRIZES, CONTESTS, ETC.

Check out other titles by The Cartel Publications

SHYT LIST 1: BE CAREFUL WHO YOU CROSS
SHYT LIST 2: LOOSE CANNON
SHYT LIST 3: AND A CHILD SHALL LEAVE THEM
SHYT LIST 4: CHILDREN OF THE WRONGED
SHYT LIST 5: SMOKIN' CRAZIES THE FINALE'
SHYT LIST 6: THE ORIGINAL BITCH OF REVENGE RETURNS
PITBULLS IN A SKIRT 1
PITBULLS IN A SKIRT 2
PITBULLS IN A SKIRT 3: THE RISE OF LIL C
PITBULLS IN A SKIRT 4: KILLER KLAN
PITBULLS IN A SKIRT 5: THE FALL FROM GRACE
POISON 1
POISON 2
VICTORIA'S SECRET
HELL RAZOR HONEYS 1
HELL RAZOR HONEYS 2
BLACK AND UGLY
BLACK AND UGLY AS EVER
MISS WAYNE & THE QUEENS OF DC
BLACK AND THE UGLIEST
A HUSTLER'S SON
A HUSTLER'S SON 2
THE FACE THAT LAUNCHED A THOUSAND BULLETS
YEAR OF THE CRACKMOM
THE UNUSUAL SUSPECTS
LA FAMILIA DIVIDED
RAUNCHY
RAUNCHY 2: MAD'S LOVE
RAUNCHY 3: JAYDEN'S PASSION
MAD MAXXX: CHILDREN OF THE CATACOMBS (EXTRA RAUNCHY)
KALI: RAUNCHY RELIVED: THE MILLER FAMILY
REVERSED
QUITA'S DAYSCARE CENTER
QUITA'S DAYSCARE CENTER 2
DEAD HEADS
DRUNK & HOT GIRLS
PRETTY KINGS
PRETTY KINGS 2: SCARLETT'S FEVER
PRETTY KINGS 3: DENIM'S BLUES
PRETTY KINGS 4: RACE'S RAGE
HERSBAND MATERIAL
UPSCALE KITTENS
WAKE & BAKE BOYS
YOUNG & DUMB
YOUNG & DUMB: VYCE'S GETBACK
TRANNY 911
TRANNY 911: DIXIE'S RISE

FIRST COMES LOVE, THEN COMES MURDER
LUXURY TAX
THE LYING KING
CRAZY KIND OF LOVE
SILENCE OF THE NINE
SILENCE OF THE NINE II: LET THERE BE BLOOD
SILENCE OF THE NINE III
PRISON THRONE
GOON
HOETIC JUSTICE
AND THEY CALL ME GOD
THE UNGRATEFUL BASTARDS
LIPSTICK DOM
A SCHOOL OF DOLLS
SKEEZERS
SKEEZERS 2
YOU KISSED ME NOW I OWN YOU
NEFARIOUS
REDBONE 3: THE RISE OF THE FOLD
THE FOLD
CLOWN NIGGAS
THE ONE YOU SHOULDN'T TRUST
COLD AS ICE
THE WHORE THE WIND BLEW MY WAY
SHE BRINGS THE WORST KIND
THE HOUSE THAT CRACK BUILT
THE HOUSE THAT CRACK BUILT 2: RUSSO & AMINA
THE HOUSE THAT CRACK BUILT 3: REGGIE & TAMIKA
THE HOUSE THAT CRACK BUILT 4: REGGIE & AMINA
LEVEL UP
VILLAINS: IT'S SAVAGE SEASON
GAY FOR MY BAE
WAR
WAR 2
WAR 3
WAR 4
THE END. HOW TO WRITE A BESTSELLING NOVEL IN 30 DAYS

WWW.THECARTELPUBLICATIONS.COM

SHYT LIST 6:
THE ORIGINAL BITCH
OF REVENGE RETURNS

By

Reign

By Reign

PUBLISHER'S NOTE:
This book is a work of fiction. Names, characters,
businesses,
Organizations, places, events and incidents are the
product of the
Author's imagination or are used fictionally. Any
resemblance of
Actual persons, living or dead, events, or locales
are entirely coincidental.

Library of Congress Control Number: 2019913046

ISBN 10: 1945240997

ISBN 13: 978-1945240997

Cover Design: Book Slut Girl

First Edition
Printed in the United States of America

What Up Fam,

Well, Hot Girls and City Boys summer is coming to a close. It was definitely one for the books. It's on to daylight savings, crisp cool fall nights and pumpkin spice. (Which I think is gross by the way). But before we totally put this summer in the rearview, we have one more release to drop!

The time you all been waiting for has arrived. "*Shyt List 6*" is here!! Yep Yvonna's back but is she the same or different? Has she grown or is she up to mayhem? It was so nostalgic reading about Yvonna again. I really did miss her and loved being thrust back into her life now. I know you will too!

With that being said, keeping in line with tradition, we want to give respect to a vet or new trailblazer paving the way. In this novel, we would like to recognize:

Chloe Anthony Wofford Morrison is a Pulitzer and Nobel Prize award Winning Novelist, Essayist, Editor, Teacher and Professor. For almost five decades, Mrs. Morrison has wowed readers with such notable works as, *"Beloved"*, *"Song of Solomon"*, *"Tar Baby"* and *"The Bluest Eye"*. Without this prolific novelist kicking down doors and paving the way, The Cartel Publications, and many other companies like it, may not have seen the light of day. We thank her for all the gifts she left with the world. May her work continue to teach and lead and may her soul rest in peace.

Aight, it's finally time...Goin' and get to it. I'll catch you in the next book.

Be Easy!

Charisse "C. Wash" Washington
Vice President
The Cartel Publications
www.thecartelpublications.com
www.facebook.com/publishercwash
Instagram: publishercwash
www.twitter.com/cartelbooks
www.facebook.com/cartelpublications

Follow us on Instagram: Cartelpublications

#CartelPublications

#UrbanFiction

#PrayForCece

#RIPToniMorrison

#ShytList6

Note To Reader:

This novel is based on **<u>Option One</u>** in *Shyt List 5*

Ocean - A Fable
By T. Styles

A woman walked toward the ocean mentally weighed with the troubles of her world. Under the moonlight she yelled, "Help me! My heart can no longer suffer the past, for the future requires my attention and I am weak."

"Easy, child," the Ocean replied. "I will lift your burdens. But never come back again, for if you do, I will make your worst nightmares real, from here until eternity."

The woman walked away and returned to her life of peace, made better by the Ocean's mercy. For a while, she reveled in serenity and did well. But a year later she had forgotten the Ocean's compassion and went back to her evil ways.

Returning for more help, she said, "Help me! My heart can no longer suffer the past, for the future requires my attention and I am weak."

The Ocean replied, "Easy, child. I will not lift your burdens. Instead, I will give you what you've always deserved."

Sniffling she asked, "And what is that?"

"My Dear Child, its Karma."

PROLOGUE
1:37 A.M.
THE PHILIPPINES

The monsoon attacked the luxury red clay-colored multi-story home, bringing with it the howling of the wind.

Wearing a long silk red robe, with a black bat on the back, Yvonna tiptoed down the hallway of her home, toward the lit bedroom off to the right of the corridor.

When she reached the doorway, she smiled at her beautiful fourteen-year-old daughter Delilah who was sitting on the window seat, the curtains behind her blowing in the breeze. Her long black hair dancing around her face, as if putting on a show for the wild air.

Smiling, Yvonna leaned up against the doorway. She couldn't get over how beautiful she had grown. She went from a little girl to getting the attention of locals who caught a glance as she walked by. She was a quiet spirit, who preferred being alone, with nothing but her computer for company.

Although she and Delilah were as different as sugar and pepper, in many ways they were similar.

For instance, they were both nocturnal.

Doing their best contemplating at night.

"You're still up." Yvonna said.

"Can't sleep."

"Well, you're going to get everything wet," Yvonna wiped her hair behind her ear. "Maybe you should close the window."

Delilah looked out and back at her. "I like the storm." As always, Delilah's voice was barely above a whisper. It was as if she preferred not being seen or heard. Almost invisible. "It makes me comfortable."

"Me too."

"And dinner was nice, momma. And I know I left the dining room before I could tell you it's just that—"

"I know…Chomps and his…behavior. I really wish things were different. We're trying to understand why he feels the need to be…so…well…violent." Flashes of the many she killed entered in her mind in that moment, bringing with it a sense of hypocrisy.

"I get it," she sighed. "But maybe it's not for you to know."

"True." Yvonna nodded, as the crackling wind grew louder. "It doesn't mean you don't deserve my attention though," she walked inside, standing in the middle of the room. "Because you're so fragile and—"

"Momma, I'm fine, really. You don't have to fuss over me."

Yvonna took a deep breath. "I know you've been sad."

She looked away. "I wish it was sadness, I really do." Delilah looked down. "To be honest I don't know what I'm feeling." She sighed deeply. "It's almost like, like, so many thoughts be going on in my head and…and…I don't know what to do."

Yvonna's heart broke with each word. It was obvious that she was also suffering from mental illness, which plagued Yvonna all her life. Did she transfer her hell onto her only child?

"Delilah, I'm so sorry."

"Oh, mommy, I wish I could be happy for you so that you wouldn't have to worry." She began to cry. "So that you can smile more and—"

"Don't say that," Yvonna ran deeper into the room. She sat next to her on the window seat, pulling her hand into her own. "My own thoughts haunt me, not you."

"You say that but you never tell me how. Tell me."

"I want you to be better and not…not…sad, but not for me, sweetheart." She touched the side of her face. "But for you. Because I know how it feels to…to…feel like you aren't yourself. To feel like you're…" Her words trailed off.

In the past, she did all she could to ignore her life in the states and that included her warped mind, made that way due to years of childhood emotional and sexual abuse.

Delilah looked at Yvonna with her whole heart. "What, mommy? Talk to me."

Yvonna released her hand. "Crazy. Like me."

"Like you?" Delilah grabbed her hand. Her eyes were wide with hope. "Mommy, you feel crazy sometimes too?"

"Stop."

"No! Tell me how you're like me so I can understand why I…why I feel like this." She placed a palm over her heart. Her hand trembled. "Please, momma."

"Delilah, not right now. We have to—"

"Momma, please!"

Yvonna took a deep breath, kissed her cheek and rose slowly. She was not willing to go back to the old days. Besides, what good would it accomplish? She was in the Philippines and most of the people who had abused her and the other children when she was a child were either dead or arrested.

She'd seen to it herself.

"Get some rest. The parade's tomorrow and you know how much you love it." Rubbing her arms, Yvonna walked toward the door.

"Mommy!"

Yvonna stopped and turned around. "Yes, Delilah."

"I'm sorry." She opened the window wider and fell three stories down.

CHAPTER ONE
SUNDAY

She couldn't leave the car. Every time she breathed, blinked or allowed a thought to enter her mind, she would be forced to see her only child falling three stories out of a window. And it ripped her soul.

Did Delilah try to hurt herself?

Or was it an accident like she claimed?

The hospital didn't believe her, and so she was remanded for a few days. All she wanted was for her to know how much she loved her. All she wanted was for Delilah to know she cared. It was one of the reasons she killed Delilah's father. It was never a love connection to begin with between them, but when he separated her from her child, Yvonna searched the world and killed many to get her back.

It ended with his death.

Throwing down the visor, she wiped the liner away that smeared along the perimeter of her eye, took a deep breath and walked outside. Her sandals sunk into the wet grass, due to the continuous raining from storms. Since brown mud now covered her shoes, she

kicked them off at the door and walked through the living room.

The moment she stepped inside, she could hear Bricks within the house talking on the phone. On the table sat a bottle of Hennessey.

He started early.

Not again. She thought.

Ever since Delilah hurt herself she felt he wasn't as receptive and she wanted more help. In her opinion, he spent more time drinking and not enough time caring and she secretly hated him for the detachment.

It didn't matter that he spent the past two days at Delilah's side in the hospital right along with Yvonna. It didn't matter that he prepared all of the meals because Yvonna could barely stand in the kitchen without crying. She was a ticking time bomb and she wanted him to do more. She wanted him to be as distraught as she was, to the point of breaking down.

At least then, she wouldn't be alone.

Walking up the spiral staircase leading to their room she pushed the door open, just as he sat the phone down on the bed. Seeing her, he drank what was left of his Hennessy and placed the glass down. "What's up?" He wiped his mouth with a squeeze to the lips. "How's she?"

She folded her arms over her chest and eyed his phone before looking at him again. "Who were you talking to?"

He dragged a hand down his face. "Fuck!"

"Fuck what?" She yelled. "I asked you a question."

"Yvonna, don't start this shit again. We've been together for years and you still don't trust me. I gave up my life for you."

"Nigga, I'm not trying to hear all that," she stormed over to his phone and snatched it off the bed. The moment she saw the 202 area code, representative of D.C., she tossed it down. "What is up with you and this...this...obsession with—"

"Home?" He said completing her sentence. "And my family? Is that what you asking?"

"Whatever, Bricks."

"Me missing home has nothing to do with my love for you." He walked up to her and rubbed her arms. Massaging her shoulder blades. "Now let's stop all this fighting. I'm not in the mood."

"No, no," she wiggled away. "You want to be anyplace but with me. You hate our lives to—."

He yanked her by the hair and tugged backwards. With her neck exposed, he sucked lightly, before running his tongue lower, between her breasts.

"Get off," she yelled, while hitting him as hard as she would if she seriously wanted to be released. The thing was, she didn't. "I don't want you touching me."

But they fucked this way before and he could take a blow, knowing that when it was all said and done, his dick would be nestled firmly inside her. As she continued to pound his shoulders, he tossed her on the bed, yanked off her clothes and pushed into her wetness.

Her pussy was like oil.

Her body was his best friend.

The moment they were connected, she let out a long moan. They argued a lot, and fought most every other night, but neither wanted to be without the other. "Damn...why you feel like the first time?" He asked. "Shit, you so wet."

She answered by covering his mouth with her own and bucking her pussy upward and downward so his entire dick could be slick. "I love you," she whispered. "I...I..."

"I know, Squeeze." He fucked her harder and with a better aim to the center so he could catch the G-Spot. "I fucking love you too."

When they were getting all the way in the mix, he pushed her legs apart and rose up and fell repeatedly like she was a bull's-eye and he was hitting the target. Yvonna nibbled on her bottom lip before sucking her own fingers. Fucking him felt like Christmas.

Flipping her over, he quickly reinserted and moved slowly at first, until he felt himself heating up. He was about to cum and knew he wouldn't last. "I'm...I'm almost there, Squeeze."

"Me too," she backed into him harder and before they knew it, all their troubles had gone away.

For the moment.

Out of breath, Bricks looked over at her. They were lying face up. "Now that you got the dick, how is Delilah?"

She shook her head in embarrassment. If there was one thing that could be said when it came to their sex game things were intact and he knew how to calm her crazy ass down.

She rolled over on her side and looked into his eyes. "The doctor says the medication he gave me won't work for her."

Bricks adjusted a little. "Oh yeah? What about going higher?"

"He says upping the dosage won't help either." She eased out of bed and slipped into her red robe.

Flopping on the edge of the bed she looked over at him. "I don't know what to do."

Bricks slipped back into his boxers and rubbed her back. "Listen, you know what we have to do."

"Bricks, stop."

"What?" He threw his arms up in the air. "I love being in this country, Yvonna. The culture. The weather when it's right. But if they can't help her sickness then maybe we should go someplace that can. Home."

"What about them?"

"Who?"

She frowned. "All the people who been trying to kill me since I left. If I go back home, Bricks, they will...they will...do just that. Is that what you want?"

"How you sound? You know I don't want anybody hurting you."

"Then what are you saying?"

"If we go back we have to be safe. That's it." He shrugged. "Even if I see my family I won't go no place but my Aunt Cora's crib. And you need to stay at any motel we rent. The moment we figure out if the doctors can help, we get her cared for and take the next plane back here."

Yvonna's heart thumped. She stood up and crawled between his legs like a child. Resting her face on his thigh, she felt at ease when he stroked her hair. "We promised never to go back." She began to cry.

"Then we won't go," he said. He hated seeing her distraught. "I don't want you doing anything you not feeling. We'll just have to find another—"

"What's that?" Her head shot up. "The fucking doorbell."

Bricks rose, shuffled a little and helped Yvonna to her feet. "You expecting company?" His gaze was intense.

She shook her head no.

They walked down the staircase and Bricks opened the door.

"What do you want, Tala?" Yvonna asked, pulling her robe closed.

Tala was a beautiful Filipino woman who sold Pastillas de leche candies to the kids in the neighborhood.

"Where is your son, Yvonna?" Tala's dark hair was pushed in a lazy bun and she was wearing a white apron that was soiled with food.

"In his room, why?" She said defiantly. "I mean, if you know something I don't just say it."

"Are you sure he's in his room?"

Yvonna frowned and heard a noise in the background. It was almost too loud to hear what Tala was saying. "Stop beating around the bush and tell us what's going on!"

When the commotion grew louder, Yvonna and Bricks quickly ran outside and up a dirt street. Her robe flew open, exposing her naked body.

She didn't care.

When they spotted a lot of activity, they hustled behind the back of a house. There they saw twelve-year-old Chomps lying on the ground and being hit in the face by a twenty-one-year-old grown man.

Livid, Bricks rushed up to the scene, shoved the man off Chomps and wailed on the twenty-one-year-old with firm fists. Before long, several bystanders alerted the neighbors that the foreigner was beating up one of their own. Within a minute, five strong angry Filipino men were rushed in their direction.

Seeing they were about to be outnumbered, Yvonna grabbed Chomps by the arm and yelled, "Bricks, come on, we have trouble!" She pulled her robe closed.

Bricks continued to pound the already bludgeoned man's face. He seemed to be transported to a dark place, that wouldn't allow him to stop his actions. And for a brief second, she wondered whom the man under his bloody fists represented in his mind.

Could it be her?

When Bricks was still going to work, Yvonna looked at the group getting closer. Some were holding pieces of wood and pipes as weapons. Others had objects too difficult to describe. But all were armed and ready.

"Bricks, let's go!"

Finally, he looked up and saw the group descending on them. Soaked in blood and easing off the young man, the trio hit it in the direction of their house. The clan was close and when Chomps tripped on his own foot and fell down, the mob almost caught them. But Bricks swooped him up and dodged inside, within moments of them being struck from behind.

Although safely in the house, that didn't stop the group from approaching their front yard, yelling the wildest of obscenities in Filipino.

"Pakshet!"

"Punyeta!"

"Tarantado! Ungas!"

As the countrymen continued to spew words of venom at the foreigners, Bricks stomped up to

Theodore "Chomps" Blake with anger. This type of thing happened repeatedly with the kid and made his life a living hell. In the Philippines, a fistfight always took the place of weapons but back home he was certain his type of behavior would earn him a bullet to the head sooner than later.

Then there was the history of the boy's dysfunctional life. Which was why he understood.

No blood relation to Bricks, he was a friend of his father who was now deceased. But the weird story surrounding his biological mother and father was horrific and explained Chomps' mood swings.

Michelle Blake had given birth to Chomps when her son, Mitch K. Blake, nicknamed "Deuce" had married his high school sweetheart Karen Dexter. Karen couldn't have children of her own and both her and Deuce wanted a child. Bet, feeling bad for her son, agreed to carry their child to full term.

Before Bet had a chance to change her mind after realizing how weird things would be to mother her son's child, Deuce and Karen went to a fertility clinic where Karen's egg was retrieved from her body and induced with Deuce's sperm.

Against the doctor's orders, the forty-two-year-old woman got pregnant and carried their baby to full term. But a week after their son Theodore "Chomps" Blake was born, Karen discovered Deuce was seeing someone else whom he planned to leave her for. Karen's entire world was rocked having walked in on them in her bedroom making love.

Karen not able to accept living without him, called him from her mother's house, who was out of town on business. Deuce agreed to meet her there to reconcile and when he walked through the door, she hugged him, cried in his arms and put a bullet through her head.

Deuce was overwhelmed with guilt and without thinking about Chomps, picked the gun up and put a bullet through his forehead. Their life story was very full and filled with secrecy.

The thing was Michelle didn't want to be a mother and through a lot of dramas, Bricks got involved.

No matter what, Bricks took to the young man like a godfather and then a father but his peculiar behavior recently started to stun him. He seemed obsessed with causing fights, stealing things that didn't belong to him and even peeping through windows to stare at girls, despite being attractive.

As the crowd continued to yell at them from inside the house Bricks sighed. "What is wrong with you,

Theodore? They could have killed you. Why you keep looking through windows?"

"She was pretty."

Bricks glared.

Yvonna walked over to the window and peered outside. The mob wanted blood. It was all in their eyes. "I think you're right, Bricks." She said in a low voice. "We need to go to the states for a little while."

Bricks walked over to her. "I don't know, babes. You sure about that? You made some good points about people being out to get you. What if—"

"I'm positive." She cut him off to stop him from saying too much. "In fact, I think we should go now."

Having caught her apprehension, Bricks walked her away from Chomps' earshot to prevent him from hearing about the history Yvonna wanted to keep from Delilah. "But your enemies," he whispered grabbing her arms. "And...and...what about the...the...women you met when you flew back to the states that time, to get money. I think their names were Mercedes and Yvette." He stepped closer. "You took their paper and came back here. How you know they won't come for you?"

"I don't." She knew he was right. "But we don't have a choice." The mob grew louder, wanting to kill everyone inside.

"I don't want to leave!" Chomps yelled, thinking about all the pretty girls left behind. They didn't know he stepped up behind them. "Please!"

"Stop being selfish," Bricks said. "This part your fault, lil nigga." Bricks looked at Yvonna and back at Chomps. "Grab what you need and leave everything else. We gonna get Delilah then we flying out tonight."

It was a beautiful day with an icy blue sky. And the small airliner headed to America was preparing to take flight.

Yvonna and Bricks sat next to each other while Chomps and Delilah sat to the left of them. Both were drinking but Bricks was on his second miniature. He seemed nervous and on edge and she wondered why.

Didn't he want to see the family he loved so much?

Every now and again, Yvonna would glance at Delilah as she sat in her seat on her laptop. She was

typing and wearing pink glitter ear buds while listening to music. She had fractured her leg from the fall and was okay, but her mind was in desperate need of repair to hear Yvonna tell it.

Delilah didn't feel the same way.

She claimed it was an accident but all she wanted was her mother to tell the truth about the past, *their* past, believing if she did she would have answers. But Yvonna's heart ached to think that Delilah was possibly going through mental illness. Surely the past would not help the child.

"Bricks," she whispered.

He didn't hear her. He was texting his family who couldn't wait to see him. Since he got on the plane he received a total of fifty messages in a family group chat and shook his head as he read each word, overcome with love.

When he felt her staring, he looked over at her but she quickly looked away.

Good, he could send one last text. So he typed:

Don't invite her

"What you doing?" Yvonna asked, causing him to rattle a little and hide his phone.

"Um…nothing…"

She rolled her eyes. "Your family is super annoying." She said shaking her head. "I hope you know that."

"They just miss me that's all. I wish you got to know them instead of automatically thinking they don't want me to fuck with you."

"They don't. The problem is I'm your wife. It's not their choice."

"Nah…it's just that…"

He was still talking, but Yvonna had zoned out on the conversation and directed all of her attention to Delilah who was still typing on her laptop.

"She'll be fine," Bricks said, sensing Yvonna's fear. "The doctor will help her."

"How can you be sure?"

"Because you've been through a lot and you deserve happiness."

You sound stupid. She thought to herself. *I'm the last person on earth who deserves happiness.*

"I'm a monster, Bricks," she said. "You and me both know it. I deserve every evil thing that can ever happen to a person and more."

He frowned, and finished the vodka in his bottle. The pretty serial killer was right. "Yvonna, I want to talk to you about—."

"Switch with Delilah right quick." She said interrupting.

"But I wanted to tell you a few things first. It's about—."

"Bricks, please." She sighed. "Whatever you want to tell me can wait. I have to prepare Delilah for the states and what she can expect. It's been a while since she'd been there. She may not remember."

He kissed her on the cheek and sighed. Next he rose and tapped Delilah. She jumped. "Your mother wants you."

She closed her glitter MacBook and sat next to Yvonna. "Momma, are you okay?" She asked with worried eyes before removing the ear buds.

"I'm fine." Yvonna looped her arm through Delilah's. "I just want you to know, that…that I love you."

"You're so silly," she said in a low voice. "I know that already."

"Seriously. You may feel like you're alone, I know you do, but you're not. I'm here with you every step of the way. And you *will* get better."

Delilah smiled and leaned her head on her shoulder. "I don't know what I would do without you."

Yvonna thought about all those she wronged in the states and shivered. Delilah being without a mother was possible for sure. "You don't have to worry about that." She was lying and she knew it. But who needed to hear the worst just yet? What good could it possibly do her now? "No matter what, I will always be with you, Delilah. That much I promise."

The plane took off on the flight toward hell.

At least the motel room was inconspicuous. In other words, it was a trashy mess.

That didn't mean that things were out of place. It was obvious that the staff did their best to make it presentable but it was in desperate need of an overhaul. New beds. New carpets. The works.

But Yvonna knew had they walked into a luxurious hotel, the type that she preferred, the million people

who wanted her dead would descend on the property with one objective in mind.

To take off her head.

After putting their clothing away, into chipped, rattling wooden drawers, Yvonna sat on the edge of the bed. Bricks sat next to her. "This place a mess." She said.

"I know." He agreed.

She looked at Chomps who was running around the room, yelling and banging on everything nailed down. It was as if he had to make noise to feel alive. They normally tuned him out but today he seemed especially excitable and that made Yvonna uneasy.

There was a knock at the door.

"I'll get it," Bricks said standing up.

She approached him. "Are you sure?" She whispered. "That...you should be opening the door since...you know?"

"We fine. Trust me. Nobody knows we're here yet. We have at least today."

When he pulled it open he saw a pretty tall girl with strawberry cream weave hair running down her back. She smiled and extended her hand. "I'm Zyla."

Bricks looked back at Yvonna who took his side. The last thing he wanted was Yvonna's jealous ass tripping. But he reluctantly shook her hand anyway. "What you want?" He asked. "We busy."

"Like I said, I'm Zyla. You guys have everything you need?"

"I guess but—."

"Good. So let me get to what I really want to know, how long you staying?"

"You work here or something?" Yvonna asked.

"Nah, but I basically live here and that means I'ma need you to keep it the fuck down."

They glared.

"Fuck you just say to me?" Bricks asked stepping closer, fearing he would have to knock her out.

"You're making noise and noise brings the police. Including myself, the people who stay here don't need all that. So respect the code, or I'ma have to teach you how." She smiled and stomped away.

"I know this bitch must be losing her mind. I should—."

Yvonna stopped him before he stormed after her and snatched her hair out the roots. Back in the day she would've yanked the girl by the sew in herself, before beating her within every inch of her life but she was worrying about Delilah these days.

It was the only reason she was there.

Yvonna closed the door and locked it with the latch. "Chomps, keep it down. You're bothering the neighbors."

He threw himself on the bed face up and crossed his arms. "I hate it here already."

"Momma, what's up?" Delilah said. "With that lady?"

"Don't worry about her." She sighed.

There was a change in Yvonna that moment.

Zyla knocking on the door stunned Yvonna and suddenly she felt the need to be a little more transparent. "But listen, there are some things you don't know about me. When I was younger, I hurt a lot of people and, well, these people may try to come after you." Chomps stood next to Delilah and she grabbed one of each of their hands. "So while we're here, you can't go anywhere else but this room. I really am sorry."

"If somebody bothering you, I'll kill 'em!" Chomps said pulling his hand back and swinging small-knotted fists.

"Easy, playa." Bricks replied. "It ain't about that. It's about being careful. And staying out of nigga's way." He gave Chomps a serious eye.

Chomps stormed away and sat on the chair by the table next to the window. What he wouldn't give to hurt something or somebody. To feel alive.

Bricks looked at Yvonna and shook his head. The boy was a mess and he knew it. But he had his whole heart.

Yvonna looked at her watch. "Okay, Delilah, let's go. Grab your jacket. It gets cold in a doctor's office."

She quickly moved toward her laptop bag. "Okay. I'm ready."

"You can't bring your laptop. You won't be there that long."

She sighed and put the bag down.

"I'll be back later," Yvonna said to Bricks.

"I love you."

She nodded and walked away. For some reason, to him, it felt like the end.

CHAPTER TWO
MONDAY

Yvonna walked into the Psychiatrist's office with her eyes shielded in shades. The room was full and it included teenage girls and boys around Delilah's age. Their parents were with them and seeing the multitude placed Yvonna on edge. In the Philippines, she could control her environment, which mainly meant just being with she and her family.

But this was different.

Too many strange faces looking in their direction gave her anxiety.

She had reason to be weary. After all, she had done many a thing in the United States, which caused her to fear for her safety.

Delilah held onto Yvonna's hand for dear life, sensing her fidgety mood. Walking up to the counter Yvonna removed her shades. "Um, excuse me, we're here for a visit."

The young black girl with a kind smile looked up at her. "Sure, your name?"

"It's actually for my daughter."

"Great. Her name?"

"Delilah," Yvonna cleared her throat, looked behind her and back at the receptionist. "Delilah Harris."

The Sweet Receptionist smiled again and looked at her computer. "Oh yes, we have you here." She grabbed a clipboard loaded with forms. "Fill these out and bring them back when you're done."

"Will it hurt?" Delilah whispered, her body trembling.

"Of course not," the Sweet Receptionist said touching her hand, which was plastered on the counter. "Dr. Amber is amazing and everything will be fine, Delilah. You're in good hands."

"Are you sure?"

"I promise."

Yvonna and Delilah walked toward two empty red chairs. Since the Pakistani woman who sat between them, refused to move so they could sit together, they had to talk over her, which was hella awkward.

Yvonna's only hope was that the doctor would be able to assess her quickly because as it stood, Yvonna had extreme anxiety.

Why was she back in the one country she hated?

Why did she allow herself to reenter the den of evil?

When she looked over at her daughter, she remembered all at once. She was there to save her child's life.

"You're not going anywhere," a mother across the way yelled to her daughter, who was wearing jeans too tight, a jacket around her waist and a red halter-top. She looked like a baby whore. "I told you not to wear that outfit."

"Mom," she said, rolling her eyes. "Leave me alone. You saw what I was wearing when I came out the house." She removed her cell phone. "So don't start tripping now."

Yvonna turned her head to the left and saw a boy who trembled every time his mother touched his arm. Was she the reason for his mental illness? The place was like a mad house in a carnival.

"I'm hungry," Delilah said softly, bringing Yvonna back to the present. "Can we get something when we leave? Maybe at a restaurant or —"

"I told you we can't go out. Remember?"

Delilah looked down at her fingertips. "You're right. I'm sorry, momma."

After the forms were returned, Yvonna sat back in her seat, looking at the door every so often. Her nervousness alerted the inconsiderate woman who remained sitting between them. "Are you okay?" The Annoying woman asked Yvonna with an attitude as if she cared. "You're giving me the creeps."

Delilah smiled awkwardly in defense. "I'm sorry, my mother is worried about me that's all."

It was partly the truth.

Mostly Yvonna was worried someone would come in and chop off her head.

"Well relax," The Annoying woman said. "You're making me uneasy. I don't like feeling uneasy when my son's back there. So—."

"Mrs. Harris," A nurse said, holding the door toward the back open. "We're ready for you."

Delilah rose and walked toward the door. "Momma, are you coming?"

"It's best if she waits out here," the Nurse interrupted. "So you can have more privacy with the doctor."

Yvonna smiled and nodded rapidly. "You'll be fine…just, say how you feel. Whatever you do, tell the truth."

Delilah nodded and disappeared in the back.

Now alone, Yvonna did her best to be still but the Annoying woman, continued to look at her as if she were crazy. So she got up and walked toward the receptionist. "Do you know how long Delilah will be?"

"I'll say about an hour and a half tops."

Yvonna nodded and looked at the clock. Only five minutes passed and with the way her anxiety was set up she didn't foresee being able to make it patiently in the waiting room. "Okay, I'm going to get her some snacks. I'll be back." She turned to walk away.

"Sure, Yvonna." The Sweet Receptionist said. "Don't worry, she'll be fine."

Yvonna's eyes grew large and she paused before slowly turning back around. "How did you...how did you know my fucking name?"

She blinked a few times. "Ma'am?"

"You said my name!" Yvonna said anxiously. "How did you know my name? I didn't tell you!"

The Sweet Receptionist looked downward. "On the sheet, from when you made an appointment. I'm sorry, is that not what you want to be called? Should I say Mrs. Harris instead?"

Yvonna felt stupid.

She wiped the sweat that formed on her brow. She was coming undone and needed to take her medication or a Valium to bring herself under control. "I'm sorry, I'm just...I mean...I'll be back." She hit it for the door.

On the way out of the doctor's office the Annoying Woman shook her head. "She takes herself a little too seriously. Ain't nobody worried about her."

When Yvonna was outside, she sat in her car and cried for no reason. Ever since she'd been back in the states she was losing control. In the past when she was out of her mind she had no idea, except for the people who spoke to her who weren't there.

Now she was fully aware that she was undone and it made her concerned that Gabriella, the personality that had been torturing her back in the day, would soon return.

The medicine she took in the Philippines kept her away.

But what would happen now that she was under such pressure?

Pushing down the visor, she looked at herself in the mirror. "Pull yourself together. You are Yvonna Harris. The baddest bitch ever." She said the words although she didn't mean them. "Okay, you can handle this. And you need to be strong for Delilah. You have no choice!"

EARLIER THAT DAY

Business was booming with a long line leading toward the counter.

Silva bolted through Cinnamon's Vegan Shop, past the employees and customers. He was moving toward the back with urgency. Besides, he felt if he didn't let loose what he had to say he would definitely explode. The white t-shirt covering his lanky frame was wet with sweat and cooled him a little as he moved.

"So you take this wheat grass and —."

"Cinnamon!" Silva yelled, cutting him off as he spoke to his wife.

Cinnamon frowned and wiped his hand with the towel on the counter. He was a tall honey vanilla colored brother with red freckles along his face. The black t-shirt he wore buckled with muscles and his designer jeans could barely hide the soft bulge between his legs.

He was definitely sexy as fuck.

Cinnamon placed the wheatgrass on the table. "What is it, nigga? You know I don't allow people back here without washing they hands."

"Can I talk to you?" Silva swallowed the lump in his throat before looking at Ginger, his beautiful wife. Her Hershey colored skin sparkled under the ceiling lights. "It's kind of private."

"Whatever you want to say to me you can say it in front of her. Now what the fuck you—"

"It's okay, honey." She increased her height by standing on her tiptoes as he lowered his upper body for a kiss on her naturally red lips. "But don't forget, whatever this is can't stop the family reunion from happening this weekend. We have a lot of people coming in town."

"I got you," he said before slapping her right ass cheek, just to watch it jiggle. The man was so enamored that he watched her until she was out of sight.

Wiping his hands on the towel again he focused back on Silva. "This better be good."

"I have some news! Some, some news you won't believe." He said excitedly, palms in his direction.

"Nigga, I was busy. Get to the fucking point before I crack your neck. Now what is—"

"Yvonna is back in town!" Silva yelled cutting him off. He stepped closer. "I saw her with my own eyes, Cinnamon! She's here! In Maryland."

Cinnamon was a confident man but upon hearing the name of the woman he thought about most days of his life, he stumbled backwards. Yvonna and he had history and she was not even aware. But it didn't make his hate for her any less. Because they were connected by one of Yvonna's earlier victims.

Dave Walters.

Before he was killed, Dave Walters was an advocate at a community center called, *Each One Teach One*. And although he was in the streets at one point and time, Dave made a promise to his mother that he would change his life for the better. He lived up to this creed and as a result, operated a community center to mentor young men and women. He was like a father to them.

It was at this center that Cinnamon was nurtured and protected. Dave preached the importance of using street smarts to build yourself and a business and because of him Cinnamon was five restaurants strong.

But that didn't mean he still didn't want her head in Dave's honor.

So, while she was away, Cinnamon and the rest of the young men from the center, met twice a year to compare the information they gained about her whereabouts. After no show, many were getting disheartened, believing she was either dead or long gone. But he alone kept hope alive knowing one day she would resurface.

And when she did, he would be waiting, to end her.

"Why did you leave her?"

"I came here first."

"Go back! And I'll call up the members of Each One Teach One. And tell them we meeting." He said, rubbing his thick hands together.

"When?"

"Tonight." He paused. "Now tell me where you saw her. Let's see how we can lure that bitch to us."

PRESENT

Yvonna sat in the doctor's office with a bag of snacks in her lap, nestled inside a white plastic bag.

She had gone to the convenience store earlier and within forty minutes was back at the office. After taking a Valium to relieve her nervous mind, she was more relaxed and eager to deal with whatever issues came her way.

But why was Delilah still in the back?

When two hours passed, she walked up to the new receptionist at the desk. She was a mean looking woman; with so many lines on her face her skin resembled strings inside a banana. "I'm sorry, do you know how much longer my daughter will be?"

"Who is your daughter?" The woman frowned and made it obvious she wasn't as pleasant as the other receptionist but Yvonna was done with judging folks. Her main concern was Delilah.

"My apologies," she wiped her long hair behind her ear. "Delilah Harris. She had an appointment earlier."

The Mean Receptionist frowned. "Delilah Harris? She left twenty minutes ago."

Yvonna felt like she'd been dropped on a rollercoaster. "What...what do you mean?"

"Like I said, she's gone."

The snack bag she was holding dropped from her hand, as she bolted out the door. Now outside, from where she stood, her head whipped left and right quickly. Her heart rate kicked up speed as she said the words she hoped she'd never have to utter.

"They know I'm here and they have my daughter! They kidnapped my daughter!"

CHAPTER THREE

The sun made an appearance and shined down on a street on 65th avenue in Landover Maryland. Where most of the members of Bricks' family waited for his arrival. This large clan included his cousins, aunts and uncles, but they all adored him like a brother.

So when word got out that he was back in town, without government approval, they closed off the entire block for a party. And since most of the homes were rented or owned by his family members, there was a grill in every front lawn. Drinks on every table at the gate and a DJ standing at the mouth of the block.

It was a celebration.

It wasn't like they had weeks to plan the event either. But you would've thought they had all the time in the world because they went all out. When it came to Bricks it was all love. When he was on the streets, every dollar he earned went back to their community.

But it wasn't just about finances. Before he went to the Philippines, he was there if they needed someone to talk to. A shoulder to cry on or the hard truth. Bricks was about his blood relatives and when Yvonna took him away, they cursed her for it.

When he finally pulled up in a cab, in front of his Aunt Cora's house, the block went wild. So many people covered the street that it was hard for the cab to drive off. Chomps was at his side, and since it was obvious that Bricks loved him dearly, he was exalted too as his son.

Chomps was in awe at the attention Bricks was getting because when they left, he was too young to understand that his father was king. But he got the picture now and loved the power.

When they finally settled down, Bricks and Chomps sat in Aunt Cora's backyard at a nice card table with matching chairs. This was a home very much loved and cared for. Every piece of grass was trimmed. The garden sitting in the front of the house was rich with colors and love so bright people couldn't help but smile as they walked by.

But the inside of the home also resonated how Cora felt about those she adored. Every inch of the walls was covered with a framed photo of a niece, nephew, and her kids. Cora herself had five children, three had passed on and the other two were in prison. But their children were in her life keeping the bond alive.

After dapping, hugging and meeting with his cousins and their spawns, they stuffed him with food, drink and love. He laughed at the old times and the new while feeling guilty that because Delilah had lost her way, he was back home.

Fully fed, it was time to talk about his life. Outside of speaking on the phone, they hadn't seen him since he left the states and wondered what became of his wife.

"You look good," Aunt Cora said, with a smile on her face. At 72 years young, you wouldn't know her age unless you looked at her hands. She was strong as an ox. "I'm so happy you're home." She gripped his hand forcefully.

"It's good to be home too. I can't even lie. If I had it my way I'd never leave."

Her eyes widened. "You really mean that?"

"You know I do."

"I'm about to play with April and 'em out front," Chomps announced, wanting to breathe air away from the adults. In his mind he had been pinned up so long in the Philippines that he needed to soar in the city that gave birth to his light.

"Don't go too far," Bricks warned with a long finger his way. "I ain't fucking around with you. I'll break your—."

Aunt Cora tapped his hand, reminding him where he was. "He's a child."

"Sorry, auntie." He winked. "Don't go too far, Chomps."

"I won't!" Chomps replied, dipping away.

He didn't believe he wouldn't wreak havoc but what could he do? Announce to the world that he was a terror on two feet, ruining his rep with his cousins already?

When he was gone, Bricks talked about everything good about life with Yvonna. He spoke of the beautiful island. The beautiful people. And the beautiful food. He left out the ugly parts, including the mob almost killing them the other day, fearing they couldn't handle the truth. He was right, every time he made mention of his wife, his Aunt Cora and Raul sneered with hate.

"Wow," Aunt Cora said. "It seems like you really happy. So what about your soul?"

He frowned. "What you mean?"

"You look condemned, nigga." Raul responded.

Bricks glared a little. He knew for a fact that Raul held his own secrets and the last thing he liked was a hypocrite. He also knew they weren't speaking about religion. They were talking about his love for a serial killer.

Before Bricks could answer someone ran up the stairs. "Your wife here!" Zamia said. "You want me to tell that bitch to go home?"

They bore witness to the beginning of their relationship. With all those she had wronged under her belt, she brought the heat on the block and they lost many a family member in her war. So in a sense they wanted her gone.

Preferably forever.

"Please stay," Aunt Cora said. "You just got here."

"She's right," a woman said in a voice so sultry, even the men she wasn't talking to couldn't help but listen. "Stay. I just got here too."

Bricks frowned when he saw Amanda. He told his family not to invite her and yet there she was in the backyard. The worst part was he still cared about her in a hood rat way. But time, life and circumstances could never allow them to be together.

Who knew what would happen in the next life?

And so, when Yvonna needed the most help, her drama was the fuel Bricks needed to 'feel' something and make a decision. Caught up in a whirlwind, he ran away to be with her.

But did he make the right choice?

Bricks stood up and walked over to Amanda. She was as beautiful as she was the day he left. Light skin. Hourglass figure. Long hair. And even longer legs. All caused his dick to jump.

But why?

He was by all accounts a married man.

"Wow, I...I didn't know you were coming." Bricks said looking down at his aunt and everyone else who was on the chat when he told them to keep his homecoming a secret. Having broke code, they all looked away.

She smiled, all white teeth in tact. "I just got here. And still, I want you to stay."

"What you want me to tell Yvonna?" Zamia asked. "I can make her go home." She cracked her knuckles, ready to break her face. "So we can have more time with you."

"No...uh...I mean...let me go see what she wants."

Everyone sighed in annoyance.

He took a deep breath and pushed past his family members. It was as if he were moving through thick brush except they were bodies instead of trees.

When he finally made it to Yvonna, the look on her reddened face let him know something was off. Way off.

Running up to her, he grabbed both of her shoulders and looked into her eyes. "What's wrong, baby? Are you hurt?" He looked her up and down. "Is Delilah good?"

Suddenly he felt stupid, temporarily believing he didn't have a family outside of his own. And now his wife was in danger.

"Delilah, they...they took her." She fell into his arms and he grabbed her closer. Her eyes so wide they dried out due to the air rushing inside of them.

Separating from her he said, "Are you sure, baby? How you...how you know?"

"I'm positive! And I...I don't know who did it." She looked fragile as she waited on him to lead her to the right place. To say the right thing to make everything better. Which in a sense would mean having Delilah back in her arms, safe from harm.

"Let me get my shit and I'm coming."

"No!" Aunt Cora said, walking up behind him. "We haven't seen you in years."

"You can be with her anytime," Zamia said. "Please don't leave! Stay with us."

"This bitch...that bitch...has ruined your life!" Aunt Cora interjected. "Her drama, her wrongs have haunted you in more ways than possible. She even took you from us! And I have asked God for you to be released from this devil." She walked in front of him, wedging her body between Yvonna and his. "Let her go handle her problems. Alone." She touched the sides of his face with her soft palms. "He has answered my prayer. But if you leave, you may never return."

Yvonna was rocked.

Of course she knew many didn't like her. And she couldn't say they didn't have reason. But still, hearing strong words of hate from people she knew he adored made her uneasy. It was like wearing shoes too tight. Squeezing on a hat that didn't fit. And stuffing an extra outfit in a suitcase that was already packed too tightly.

At the end of the day, she didn't belong.

"Don't disrespect my wife. You — ."

"Bricks." If she loved him, she had to let him go. "Bricks, I — ."

Yvonna's sentence was cut short when a large screech sounded on the street. Everyone paused to see what cause the sound.

And when Bricks ran toward the source, his family moved out of his way. It was worse than he thought. There, in the middle of the concrete, laid Chomps' body.

Devastated he ran toward him and lifted him in his arms. He and the rest of his family ran after the ice cream truck that peeled away from the scene. It was pink, with black butterflies and it seemed off for a truck selling treats.

And yet because of it, Chomps was on the ground.

CHAPTER FOUR

The wind was strong. The kind with enough strength to knock over trees, throw loose structures around and even blow away a house.

Still, as the wind howled for the person known as Yvonna Harris to go away, it didn't stop her from walking up the eight steps it took to reach Jabar's door in Washington D.C.

With her weight, each step rattled and yelled, for her to leave but nothing stopped her focus.

Knocking on the loose burgundy door, it took Jabar all of fifteen seconds to open it wide. His lower half wrapped in an overused off white towel, he was cool at first but stumbled backwards when he saw Yvonna's pretty face.

Jabar wasn't as refined as some of the men who wanted her in the past. At the end of the day he was a thug, but nothing took away from his looks. With a five o'clock shadow, and solid build, the man was handsome.

"Jabar...I...I know I'm the last person you want to see but—."

"Yvonna…" he said, as if saying her name out loud, would make things realer. He wiped his hand down his smooth beard and folded his arms across his chest. Prior to now he believed the rumors were true and she was dead.

He thought wrong.

"Yes, I…I know you haven't seen me in a while."

The wind whipped her long black hair in her face momentarily hiding her features. It didn't matter. He knew who she was because she was the only woman who ever broke his heart.

"How are you?"

His arms dropped at his sides. "What you doing here?"

"I need your help."

"Jabar, fuck is you doing?" A short something about five feet asked as she stepped into the doorway. She was wearing nothing but an old, crooked wig on top of her head. At the same time, her body was stacked, making it known right away why he chose her for the day.

"Who is this?" She asked him. "We were busy."

"Go to the room," he responded, not bothering to look down at her. Besides, he couldn't move his eyes if he wanted, Yvonna's beauty required all of his attention.

"But you were just about to eat my pussy since I hooked you up first. Don't be trying to —"

"Get the fuck in the room, crab!" He yelled, pointing over her head. "Now!"

She rolled her eyes, folded her arms over her tiny breasts, and stomped bare feet out of view. Stiff thick ass refusing to bop along the way.

Yvonna stepped closer. "Jabar, somebody, somebody has my daughter."

"What you mean has your daughter?" He asked through clenched teeth.

"I know it sounds crazy, and I wish I knew more. All I can say is that they took her from the doctor's office. Probably looking for me and I don't know what to do. I need your —"

"You a user."

She took one step back after sensing his rage. "Jabar, I —."

He glared. "Ain't no need in lying or saying my name like I don't know it already." He stepped out, his bare feet standing on the gritty wooden deck. "I know who you are. When you want something, when you want revenge, you don't care who you use to get it."

Many years passed and he was still as hurt as he was the day she broke his heart.

The saddest part of the story was simple.

Yvonna used many, some who stayed around much longer and had more to lose. But to her they were all the same, a means to revenge, and she didn't care whom she hurt to reach her goal.

But Jabar, well, he was different.

Maybe she did care.

"Jabar, I'm so sorry." She wiped tears away and touched his arms. "I was young and immature and didn't deserve your love."

He pulled away from her hold but it was hard. "Now you say what I want to hear. The thing is it's too late." He walked into the house and slammed the door.

Devastated, Yvonna walked up to it and banged heavily with two fists. "Jabar!" She wept, her forehead resting on the wet wood. "Fucking open the door and talk to me! Please!"

When the door opened again, both he and the Little Naked One were pointing .45 handguns in her face.

She got the message and backed up.

"Get out of here."

She didn't move.

She knew she should but she needed a man with power to assist her in the journey. "Jabar, please don't —."

He cocked. "If you think I'ma say it again, you don't know me after all."

Defeated, Yvonna walked down the corridor toward her motel room. Her temples throbbed thinking of her life. Bricks was at the hospital with Chomps. Jabar threatened to kill her. And she was childless and alone in America.

She was almost at her door, when a pretty tall brown skin girl with bohemian locs bolted out of her room. At first she didn't recognize her until she remembered she came over earlier that day. Her hair was different. And she was arguing with a tall man with a baldhead and muscular upper body.

Yvonna paused to eavesdrop a little.

"You got five days two pay me for the other shit or we done!" He yelled pointing a long finger in her face.

"You know I'm good for it," she responded. "I got customers coming later and everything."

"I don't want to hear all that. I want my fucking money, Zy." He stepped closer. "Don't make me come back for you again." He stomped away, bumping past Yvonna on the way to his car.

Yvonna figured she was a drug dealer or involved in prostitution. After all, who could afford to change their hair so quickly when it was still fresh? "Fuck you looking at?" Zyla asked.

It was at that time Yvonna realized she was staring. "Sorry...I...nobody." She walked away and entered her room.

Now alone, she dropped to her knees and cried. It seemed to be all she could do these days. She had never; ever expected returning to America would cause her daughter harm.

After calling Bricks' cell phone and the hospital to find out if Chomps was okay, and not being able to reach him, she was growing more worried. She thought of going over to Aunt Cora's but she saw a few of his cousin's hands hover over their hips on the pop up. They were all eager to kill if anyone gave the word.

No, if she wanted to help Delilah she had to focus.

So, she decided to try to remember those she wronged the most. The list was long but the first person she called was a man whose house she stayed in for a week when she was trying to get at Swoopes. He offered his home and she gave him her ass to kiss when she was done.

When the caller answered she took a deep breath. "John..."

"Who is this?" Grogginess was heavy in his voice.

"Before I tell you who I am, I want you to know how sorry I am that...that...I hurt you. I mean, I know you had been with your wife for—"

"Ten years." He yawned. "I was with my wife for ten years when you came into my life and lied to me, making me think you wanted to be with me."

He knew who she was, and was as hurt as the day was long. She finally understood the ramifications of using her beauty for evil. "I'm so sorry. It's just that I—.""

He laughed softly, interrupting her sentence. "You know, I always made a promise to myself, that if I ever saw you I would kill you and everybody you love. So knowing this, knowing how much I hate your guts, do you still want to see me?"

She hung up and took a deep breath. For all she knew he could have taken Delilah. She would have to check to make sure.

Yvonna felt hopeless before, but she never felt as hopeless as she did at that moment. She was so caught up in the mystery that when her watch dinged, she realized she hadn't taken medicine. When she went to look for the bottle she couldn't find it.

"Oh no, oh no!" She paced the room and opened and closed every available drawer. "Please, not this, not this!"

She dropped on her knees and began to crawl on the dingy motel carpet. When she found the bottle under the bed on its side, she breathed a sigh of relief. Clutching it in her hand, she cried heavily. She had been dependent on the drugs since she left for the Philippines, this part was true, but it mainly was because she was afraid.

Afraid old friends and old evils would come back and rock her world if she went off medication.

And by that she meant none other than Gabriella.

Opening the bottle, she held the top in one hand and three pills in the other. If she took the pills, her nerves would be quieted immediately. But if she

didn't, within time, maybe she would...well...get the energy she needed to fight back.

So she stopped to think, what should she do?

CHAPTER FIVE

There was no room for other visitors.

Bricks' family had crowded the waiting room as all sat on pause for word on Chomps. His aunt right at his side, she took the liberty to bring him back from the deep end several times when she saw him mentally falling apart.

After what seemed like an eternity, the doctor walked up to him, and each of his family members rose, flanking his sides. "Doctor..." He whispered. His eyes bloodshot red. "How...I mean...is my son okay?"

The doctor, a black man with salt and pepper hair smiled. The gesture was out of place. "He'll be fine."

Bricks gasped in relief and his family members touched him.

And then the doctor's mood change. "The boy had bruises on his face. Like from a fight. Why?"

Bricks thought about the man beating him up back in the Philippines. "Oh...boys will be boys."

"I hear that, but because he was hurt today, Child Protective Services will need to talk to you." And on queue, a white woman with a clipboard stood at the doctor's side. "I really am sorry. But a truck struck him from what I'm told, with a sea of adults watching. And quite frankly, I'm worried for the boy's health. So I have a lot of questions."

Bricks heard him but he couldn't keep his eyes off the woman with enough power to change his world. After all, no blood bound him and Chomps. Although she wasn't police, when you lived a life steeped in murder, pain and revenge, the last thing you needed was an authoritative figure asking questions. But he had no choice.

He loved the boy.

So he was forced to play by the rules.

Bricks was asleep until Amanda rolled over a speed bump on his street. He wiped his eyes and looked around angrily. Sitting up, his head jerked around as his vision became clearer. "Why you bring me back? I told you I gotta go see 'bout my wife at the motel."

"Bricks," she placed a hand on top of his. "Don't go tonight. That CPS lady really had you going. You were stressed the fuck out. I mean, maybe you should get some sleep first."

He pulled away. "It ain't the fact that she had me stressed, it's that she trying to act like I'm unfit. Like I ain't got no right to him. It's 'cause of me that boy still alive. I mean...I just need to see about my wife right now and I'll worry about that later. She don't even know what's going on."

"I'm sorry. I didn't mean it like that...it's just that...I know you hurting and Yvonna, she, she always got something going on, Bricks. Maybe being around your family will be the best right now."

He frowned and smiled sinisterly. "They put you up to this shit didn't they? They always controlling me."

"Be glad you got people always looking out for you."

At that moment, his car door opened and his family members, led by his oldest cousin Raul, yanked him out of the car. Bricks was kicking and throwing fists but it didn't matter. They gained control over him and as a result he was taken into Aunt Cora's against his will.

Once in the house, they tossed him on the sofa and stood over his body. It was ten of his cousins, cramped in a living room that wasn't built for more than five comfortably.

"Can ya'll tell me what the fuck is going on?" Bricks yelled looking at Raul.

He shrugged. "You ain't been thinking straight ever since you got up with that bitch." Bricks rose and Raul said, "Sit down, killa. I'm not done talking to you yet."

Bricks complied and wiped a hand down his face. They had him outnumbered and he knew it. "What...is...this...about?"

Suddenly the line his cousins were holding broke down the middle so Aunt Cora could walk through and sit next to him. Her soft wrinkled hand touched his thigh. "Son, you staying right here."

He glared. "That ain't happening, auntie. You know that."

"I understand why you *think* you gonna leave, but with what's going on out in the streets, with your wife, I'm not gonna be able to let you do that."

He glared and his expression looked as if he were about to do his aunt harm and so Raul and two of his cousins charged, to pin him on the sofa. "Fall back, Bricks." Raul warned pressing his body into the

cushions. "Don't make me fuck you up." He pointed at him.

"Fuck is you doing? I would never hurt my aunt!" He tried to wiggle out of his grasp but nothing.

"Let him go." Aunt Cora said calmly.

They quickly complied.

Bricks was so angry he was trembling. There was nothing like being held against your will so he was suffering badly.

"Bricks, son, like I said, you're staying here." She continued. "And I know how you feel about that woman, so I called a family meeting to see to it my wishes are met."

His eyes fell on Amanda, who walked inside. Her facial expression showed she was riddled with guilt.

"Why you doing this, Aunt C?" Bricks asked calmly. "This ain't right. If somebody woulda kept uncle Perry from you when them niggas broke into your house you would've lost it."

"True." She nodded. "But where your uncle Perry at now?"

He was dead.

"The city is after your girl," Raul said stepping closer. "And we made an agreement that we would keep you out the line of fire. That way you can survive. Otherwise the hit is on you too."

"Let me get this straight, you basically sanctioned a hit on my wife's life!" Bricks yelled. "My wife, nigga!" He pounded a fist on his chest. "There's a difference. She ain't this bitch standing right here! Our marriage makes her one of us!" He pointed at Amanda.

"Never." Zamia said.

"That may be true about her being your wife," Aunt Cora started. "But it won't change my decision. Now every killer with a means to make a little dough is looking for your wife's pretty little face. And when they find her, I don't want mine nowhere near."

Bricks was fuming. "This is wrong," he whispered, having the energy wiped out of him due to not being able to break free. "She gonna think I abandoned her. She gonna think I don't love her."

"I'm sorry about that too," She said. "I really am."

He knew his family well enough to know that if he tried to make a move for the door, the scene would get violent. If he wanted things to go his way, he had to be smart. Love could be dangerous with sudden moves.

After staring at the floor, slowly his eyes rose and met each of theirs. "Ain't nothing I can do now."

Most of his cousins smiled in relief but Raul knew him well enough to know he wasn't relenting. Something was up.

"That's good, son."

"I'm not done." He stared at them all. "You need to know ain't nothing gonna stop me from getting back to that woman."

"Nigga…we wouldn't have it any other way," Raul nodded with a smile. "You a Thomas." He stepped closer. "But you still ain't getting out this house, my nig. Period."

CHAPTER SIX
TUESDAY

The weather was gloomy and Mother Earth was yet again threatening rain. Just like in the Philippines, it was almost as if a storm was following Yvonna Harris. Bullying her to leave.

She had taken pills the night before to keep Gabriella away and now it was the next day. Which meant she was rattled all over again. Sitting outside in front of the doctor's office in a rental, double-parked, Yvonna did her best to calm her nerves but nothing worked.

She'd been walking around with her cell phone, pushing a picture of Delilah into the face of anyone who gave her a minute. Stranger after stranger, all said what she feared, that not only had they not seen her, but they could care less.

Normally Bricks would soothe her mind, fuck her brains out and bring her back to focus. But since he was nowhere to be found, she had to endure another day alone.

She needed him. He was also her best friend. And she was certain that his family was filling his ears with

By Reign

vile opinions of the woman she used to be, and to be honest, she understood.

But that was then.

Yvonna, despite what they thought, had proven herself to be a dutiful wife and mother. Loving. Caring. Even to Chomps. She cooked every night, took care of them when they were sick and loved them when they felt low.

So where was the cavalry when she needed them most?

When she loosened up a little, she grabbed her black leather purse from the passenger's seat. Pushing the contents inside around, including her anxiety medicine and gum, she reached for her last Valium wrapped in a paper towel. She searched the car for water but when she found none, she swallowed it dry, allowing the oval shape object to bang along the insides of her windpipe as it trailed down.

Giving it a few more moments to work, she pushed open the door and walked inside.

And then she saw the last person she wanted to face.

The Mean Receptionist.

Placing her warm hands on the cool counter, she looked down at the woman.

Be nice, Yvonna.

"Excuse me...I need...well I need some help."

The Mean Receptionist slammed down the chart she was viewing and in agitation, gave her angry attention. "What can I help you with today, ma'am?" The question may have appeared to be professional, but the tone was aggressive. And it was obvious she didn't like the ground Yvonna stood on and the feeling was mutual.

"Yes, I, um...I have a request that...well...it's sort of unique. Because, I can't get the police involved."

She rolled her eyes. "Ma'am, I have other people waiting. So what you want? Because unfortunately for you, I don't have all day."

Yvonna looked back, and sure enough, four people walked up behind her waiting to get assistance. So she stepped closer to the counter, lowered her head and whispered, "My daughter went missing, after leaving this office, and I need the names of every patient here that day."

The woman frowned and remained silent.

"Ma'am, did you...did you hear me? I need the names of – "

"I don't know what you're trying to imply, but we certainly didn't have anything to do with a child going missing." She was loud for show. "Now you can—"

"Can you hurry up?" A small white lady holding the hand of a tall black boy said to Yvonna. "We have an appointment in a minute." She looked at her watch. "One that we've been waiting on for over six months. We—"

"Just a little while," Yvonna smiled nervously at the woman. She suddenly had a sense of falling and wondered why the Valium wasn't working. Facing the Mean Receptionist she said, "If I could just see the list of all the patients here the day my daughter went missing, I could—"

"I don't know who you think I am, but I will not be giving you anything of the kind. And if you really believe something happened to your child, your first line of defense should be the police."

"I understand but I can't...I can't call them."

"Why?"

"I just can't..."

"Well that sounds like a personal problem because I have a room full of people waiting."

"Exactly," the short woman with the tall child added. "So hurry up and get out the way."

"You heard her," the Mean Receptionist said. It was like she was being jumped. "Get out the way or you won't have to worry about the police. Because I'll call 'em for you."

It was no use, she wouldn't get the help she was seeking.

Slowly she backed away from the counter, bumping into a few people on the way out. As soon as the door closed behind her, she was hit with another blow. It was obvious in that moment how much the world really hated her.

Looking in the direction she doubled parked, she saw her rental car gone.

Her eyes widened. "No, no, no, no!" She touched the sides of her face with warm palms. "Please, please don't be gone. Don't be gone!" She walked briskly around the lot, hoping she parked the car some place else and not in the tow away zone like she remembered. Her reason for leaving the car there was simple, she was only going in for a second. And now she realized how truly stupid she was.

She was running around in circles in the lot, when the Sweet Receptionist walked up to her and smiled. Her presence calm. "Mrs...ma'am, are you okay?"

Yvonna was too hysterical to see her at first. Being overwhelmed with grief caused everything to appear in a blur, as if in a dream. So the young lady touched the sides of her face softly. "Mrs. Harris, can I help you?"

It's amazing how far a little kindness could go. Because just seeing her face gave Yvonna a blanket of peace. Shaking her head slowly from left to right, as huge drops of tears exited her eyes she mouthed the words, "My car...my purse...all of them are gone."

The Sweet Receptionist touched her heart. "I'm so sorry. Come with me." She held out her hand. "I'm on break. I may be able to help."

Yvonna couldn't move. The Valium had kicked in at the wrong time. And so she felt heavy, as if carrying a thick child on her shoulders.

"Mrs. Harris..." she softly grabbed her hand. "Come with me. Please, I want to...I want to help you."

A few minutes later, Yvonna was lying in one of the beds in an empty patient room. The Mean Receptionist had many problems with the temporary arrangement, from the fact that it was unprofessional, to simply not liking Yvonna. But the Sweet Receptionist put her job on the line. Not only that, but she also held a secret against the Mean Receptionist that she didn't mind using if she bucked.

And it had everything to do with the woman tapping the petty cash fund more than a few times.

After thirty minutes of allowing Yvonna to rest, the Sweet Receptionist entered the room.

Yvonna sat up and wiped her eyes. She did feel better, although nothing changed in her life. Delilah was still gone. "I want to say…just…thank you."

She smiled. "No need. I…" she dug into her pocket. "Here. I want to give you this." She handed her twenty dollars. "I would give you more but it's all I have."

Yvonna was overwhelmed with her warmth. She wondered where she would be if more people treated her the same earlier in life. Maybe so many would not have had to fall by her hands. "I don't know why you're doing this but—"

"I feel like, it was my fault."

"What…why?"

"I told your daughter she would be fine and…something happened to her. I was on lunch but still. It makes me sad that you're in so much pain."

"Listen, everything that happened yesterday was on me."

"I don't know if it's true but I still need to help. Someone did the same for me when I was trying to escape a very mean person, who happened to be my ex-husband. I kinda want to pay it forward." She took a deep breath and removed her phone from her purse. "I called an Uber for you. He's driving a gray Prius. Of course it's paid for already so you don't have to worry."

"I will never forget you."

"Just pay it forward."

CHAPTER SEVEN

Yvonna was inside a gray Prius.

The Valium she had taken was relentless and so once inside the car, she fell asleep. When she awoke, the driver, a black man in his early twenties was driving on a winding road, woods to the left and right of him. The sun had gone down long ago and the moon had taken her place and appeared to be frowning at Yvonna. As if it wanted to spit in her face.

Yvonna wiped her eyes. "Excuse me, where we, where you taking me?"

He looked back at her and she jumped when she saw his missing eye. It was stitched up badly and gave him a creepy vibe. "I'm taking you to the spot." His voice was heavy. Like nails running across a sore throat.

Yvonna looked around from inside the car, but there were no signs, or indicators that she was going the right place. She couldn't even remember where she told him to take her. "Wait…where…where is that?"

"I'm Quay."

She didn't get an answer. "Where you taking me?" She studied the features of his face again. The neat

dreads that sat on top of his head in a bun stunk like sewage. She wondered how something so in order could smell so foul.

"You know you asked to be in my car right?" He frowned and then smiled, as if she didn't catch his initial reaction. "I didn't invite you."

She scratched her scalp. She couldn't remember. Why couldn't she remember?

"Yes, I know, the, the girl, she ordered me a car."

"So why you tripping then?"

Silence passed between them as she studied the inside of the vehicle. The small pieces of lint on the floor could do nothing to defend herself if he acted violently. She needed a weapon.

"You got money?" He asked.

She frowned. "The girl...back...at the doctor's office said she paid already."

"You told me that. But this ain't no Uber. I think you hopped into the wrong car."

Oh no!

Her eyes widened. Fear struck her like knife blades all over. "But...but you...you...took me. If you ain't a Uber why take me?"

"Like I said, because you slid in my car. And you looked high." He continued to drive. "But now since we thirty miles out, far from where I scooped you, you gotta pay to go back."

She hated him. "So you always take people way out when you want something?"

"You were sleep. I ain't wanna wake you so I just drove." He shrugged. "I mean, I could let you out but you sure you wanna walk this dark road alone?"

"Pull over." She demanded.

"It's dark. Could be dangerous for a pretty thing like you."

"Open the fucking door," she threatened with her entire existence. In fact, the rage she used upon giving the demand was the first time she felt like the old Yvonna Harris. The one born and raised in southeast Washington D.C.

He pulled over, gravel crackling under the weight of his tires. Once parked, he unlocked the door, letting her out. She was about to say thanks but he pulled off quickly and she watched the car until it was out of sight placing her in pitch darkness.

The night was so black; she couldn't see her hands in front of her face. She almost felt dizzy. When she moved, her own footsteps startled her. "What's happening to me?" She said to herself, unable to believe the state of her life.

With nothing else to do, she began to walk and at first bumped into trees because she couldn't see. But after turning around slowly, she could feel the smoothness of the ground beneath her feet. Hooting in the distance. Branches crackling. All did horrors for her anxiety.

When she saw a car coming back after five minutes, she waved profusely. It was the Prius. The one that had led her down this path to begin with.

Oh fuck.

With a grin on his face, he pulled alongside her. She stared at him from a far as he rolled down the passenger side window. "If you suck my dick I'll take you back. Won't take but a few minutes. I cum quick. What you—"

"Get the fuck out my face!"

He laughed and pulled off again, throwing her back into complete darkness.

Of course she was scared, but she would rather walk than be raped, murdered and ridiculed. She had done that enough to last a lifetime. Being sexually abused was the main reason she was mentally fucked up.

She was further up the road when another car, a red pickup truck, stopped alongside her. An older black woman with a bald patch on the top of her graying head rolled the window down. She was wearing overalls and smelled of oil and dirt. But the pickup truck she was driving was in pristine condition.

"Need a ride?"

"Please." She quickly hopped inside.

They were silent for five minutes, neither saying anything outside of Yvonna's thank you. Oddly enough, it was she who said the next words. "Where...where were you going? When you picked me up?"

"Why are you out here?" The woman asked but then received a text message. She hid it from Yvonna's view when she responded while driving.

"I...there was an Uber and...you know what, it's a long story." She took a deep breath.

"Those are the only ones I got time for. Jewels fall in the details." Another text came through and she responded, again hiding the message.

"Are you busy?"

The woman shrugged. "Outside of driving I'm cool." She put the phone down. "So talk to me. Tell me what's going on in—."

"My daughter's missing and...I don't know...I don't know who has her."

The woman frowned. Her situation was more serious than she thought. "Is she living that hateful of a life where people want to see her harmed?"

"No, but I am." Yvonna turned away and thought of the many people she killed. At present, it was well over one hundred. It all started when her heart was broken due to finding out the love of her young life slept with her best friend, resulting in a son who would later be named Bilal Jr., his namesake.

After that betrayal, many paid the price for her pain.

"No judgment, I mean look at me." She shrugged. "After working as a mechanic in an old shop, I meet men off this roadway for sex and we fuck in the woods." She sighed. "When I'm done, I go home to my husband who's dying of HIV. The tragedy is, I gave it to him and while his body can't handle it, mine is doing fine. They say evil doesn't die. I think it's true."

Yvonna frowned but felt slightly better about her life.

"But I will tell you this, from someone who wronged many, and will probably wrong many more, until you live a life of grace, the worst will continue to haunt you, until you can take no more." She continued. "You will never have peace."

"What if you want to stop but can't?" Yvonna asked sincerely.

"Then get comfortable with hell."

Both women were treacherous, that much was true.

So they remained silent swimming in their own thoughts.

Thirty minutes later they were in front of the police station. Yvonna didn't want to go inside, but she felt there was no other recourse. Even if they locked her up, there would be people out looking for her only child.

At least she hoped so.

"Thanks again," she said.

The woman waved. "Remember what I said. Nothing changes before you do." Yvonna nodded and moved down the walkway as the trucker drove off. Feeling further away from finding Delilah than ever, she took another step toward the precinct.

"You going about things the wrong way." A voice said from behind. "But you're smart, so Ming's just telling you what you already know."

Yvonna paused.

She felt dizzy.

Almost as if she were floating.

She was so stunned upon hearing the voice she knew as much as her own that she was stricken with fear. Because two things were evident. First, if she was hearing voices she was losing touch with reality. Again. And second that the voice belonged to someone dead.

Slowly she turned around and the moment she saw her face, she slammed a hand over her mouth and cried.

"Don't be so dramatic," She said. "It's just little old Ming."

Before she was killed as a result of Yvonna's war, Ming Chi was the baddest nail designer in Maryland. Once enemies, the two became friends and Yvonna missed her terribly. She was one of the reasons she changed.

She removed her hand from her mouth. "But you're...you're not here."

"True. But you been seeing things that aren't there for years. And now you don't want to see Ming?" She spit on the ground. "Phooey!"

"I don't see things anymore," Yvonna pointed at her. A few people saw the beautiful woman talking to herself and shook their heads as they entered and exited the station. "I stopped, I mean, I haven't been seeing things for years until today. I've been living a life full of —"

"That's a lie and you know it," Ming stepped closer.

"You don't know me anymore." She stepped backwards, her eyes on the ground. "I've been a housewife. I've been a mother. I've been…good. You —"

"Aw, Yvonna, Ming doesn't feel like telling you the truth but you too far off to see."

"Shut up."

"The woman named Tala, who came to you the day Chomps got into a fight in the Philippines died a year earlier. And yet you saw her at your door."

"That's a lie. Bricks saw her too."

"Ummmm, no he didn't." Ming stepped closer. "The man who accompanies his son as he cares for your land on Saturday. Not real. Your favorite person at the grocery store, who always points out the best fruit since you've never been good at picking, also fake. Everybody, even me after I died, a part of your imagination."

Yvonna backed away, eyes still on the woman she once considered a friend. If she believed every word she said, would she descend further into madness?

Turning around, she moved toward the precinct, with faster steps.

"Are you stupid?" Ming yelled, her accent thicker. "If you go in there, you will not find Delilah. She will be lost! Forever."

Yvonna paused, back in her direction.

"You killed cops and gotten away with murder. 'Cause stupid police could not make things stick. But they will get back at you."

Yvonna sighed. "Stop it."

"You have people who looking for you, 'cause at one point you use them. And they filed reports. And reports turn into warrants." Ming stepped closer. "If you go in there, you will not receive help. And Ming will be sad."

Yvonna didn't go any further but she couldn't face who she deemed to be a ghost. "I don't know where to start. Where do I go to find Delilah when the enemy list is never-ending?"

"At least you're being honest. Now look at Ming, bitch. Please."

Yvonna slowly turned around and Ming smiled. She was such a cutie pie. For that moment, real or fake, Yvonna's heart warmed. Who cared if she was "seeing things" if she was feeling loved? Maybe that's why some people preferred to remain crazy.

"Good…now let's talk about plan."

"You can't help me because you're…not here."

"If Ming not real, that means you can take Ming wherever you go. What's better than that?"

CHAPTER EIGHT

ifteen minutes later they were walking toward the motel room, Yvonna was in deep conversation with Ming.

They were two long lost friends.

Hearing the commotion and needing a distraction, Zyla walked out of her room to fake like she wanted ice. Which everyone knew the kids pissed on for fun in the hopes that someone would eat it. All she was really doing was being nosey.

Standing by the ice machine, empty brown bucket in hand, she was shocked. She was watching Yvonna who appeared engrossed in a heavy convo, even laughing a few times with herself. As she stared at her with her full attention, she began to glare.

Running back into her room she slammed and locked the door behind her. Inside were large brown boxes stacked to the ceiling, along with her best good friend, an elderly woman of sixty years who was sitting on the bed.

"Where the ice? Thought we were drinking Everclear."

"You know I just made that up to see what that bitch was up to." She wiped her bohemian locs over her shoulder and sat the bucket on the floor. "But something's up with her." She pointed. "She was actually talking to herself. Now I expect that from someone your age but she something else. Too young to be crazy. Right?"

Marge frowned and shrugged. "This a dirty motel. Why you surprised?"

"It's not about surprise. I actually...look...we don't need her kind around here."

Marge laughed.

Zyla stepped closer. "Why do I get the impression you ain't feeling me? If you don't..." She rushed over to the corner where five large brown boxes sat. "...Let me remind you what we're dealing with." She opened one of the boxes and grabbed a fist full of bundled hair in plastic wrap. "If the police come by because of her, they gonna see all this stolen shit. You really want that chick ruining everything we built?"

Marge laughed. "Oh yeah...call the police wagons because somebody over there talking to they self." She opened the bottle of liquor. "I'll enjoy my shit alone. You too uptight."

"We got stolen hair in here! And you laughing, Marge?"

She took another gulp. "Child, sit down."

"Don't forget people pay $200 a bundle for this shit. All it takes is the cops coming here to collect her ass and seeing activity from our room instead."

"Listen, even if they come, we good. Besides, how much trouble can one woman who talks to herself get us into?"

Yvonna was lying on her side, with Ming sitting behind her on the bed. She had just returned from walking around the neighborhood looking for Delilah, only to come up with no information yet again.

"You need help. You alone. Not good."

"Stop telling me things I already know." Yvonna rolled her eyes.

"You need to relax too."

"And how do I do that?"

"Let's have fun."

"I'm not in the mood."

"Then let's change that." Ming stood in front of her. "What else you gonna do? Stay here and die?"

Bricks was lying on the bed, with his back faced the door. Several of his family members, including his Aunt Cora, came inside trying to get him to eat.

He refused.

All he wanted was to be with his wife and help find her daughter. He was also greatly concerned about her life. Would the people who wanted her dead make good on the threats? If only he could help, if nothing else to go over a plan but he was shut in. His family was serious. Until the threat known as Yvonna Harris was eliminated, they didn't want him anywhere near her.

There was a knock at the door. "Bricks, it's me."

He sighed deeply but kept his back in her direction.

The door opened and Amanda walked deep into the room. "I know you're angry with me."

"Anger doesn't begin to describe how I feel."

"I get it, but…I just want you to know I've been visiting Chomps."

He turned around. Now he was interested. "How is he?"

"He's going to your Aunt Shonda's house tomorrow." She sat on the edge of the mattress. "Have you seen him?"

"Talked to him on Face Time on Raul's phone." He shrugged. It wasn't good enough. "But it ain't the same as being there."

"She said she won't let the foster care system get him. Wanted me to tell you not to worry. She's already filed. If it doesn't work they'll kidnap him."

This was the part of his family he loved.

And then he thought about how they kidnapped him.

"I'll call her later."

She nodded. "Can I help you, Bricks?"

He chuckled once. He didn't trust her in the least.

"I'm serious, Bricks. I mean," she looked down and her hair draped the sides of her face. "I feel so bad about this. It's been a long time since I've been around your family and I…"

"You forgot how they could be." He said, finishing her sentence.

"Yes. I mean, I get that they want you safe but — ."

"It's not they fucking place to keep me safe." He sat up and walked across the room, leaning against the wall. "I'm a grown man. And you don't take a grown man and force him...force him...to...to...not be able to take care of his wife." He was so angry he trembled. "I love my people but I'm trying my best not to hate them for this shit right here." He looked up at her. "I need your help."

She nodded and looked down. "I can try to get you out but, but, I don't think it'll be possible." She cleared her throat and lowered her voice. "Even now someone's standing outside the door."

Bricks knew already, but hearing it was extra annoying. He sat next to her on the bed. "I know what you can do for me."

She gave him her undivided. "Anything."

"Pull out your phone. I'ma give you the details."

CHAPTER NINE

Yvonna woke up on the floor of the motel, several bottles of liquor around her. She drank herself into a hole that she hadn't been inside for many years. When she opened her mouth, her tongue tasted as if she'd been smoking and it made her stomach uneasy.

It was time to search again.

She was stirring around on the filthy carpet and trying to get up. Unable to move, when she turned her head to the right she saw Gabriella standing in the corner of the room. She was wearing an all black cat suit and looked as young as the day she first haunted Yvonna. Although off balance, she hopped to her feet, afraid of her own mind.

Wiping her eyes she said, "What...I mean...you...this...this isn't real. None of this is real." She backed into the dresser.

"You a mess." Gabriella responded.

"She's better than she was yesterday," Ming interjected, from the other side of the room.

"Shit in a cup doesn't make it chocolate milk." Gabriella switched toward Ming and stared her up and down. "Don't believe me? Get a cup, shit in it and tell me how it tastes."

"Get out Ming's face."

"Why are you here?" Yvonna interjected.

She turned around and walked toward her. "Do you mean, why did you call me? Because I only come when you need me the most." She threw her hands up. "And guess what, beautiful, I'm here! So what do you want from *me*?"

Yvonna flopped on the edge of the bed. "I never asked for you. I...I spent the last few years trying to get you out my mind. You've been nothing but trouble."

"Trouble." Gabriella glared. "I'm that part of you that deep down, knows who you really are. I mean I know it's fucked up." She shrugged. "Who wants to admit the darkest part of themselves? And still I say, you are just that, a serial fucking killer."

"We don't need her," Ming said.

"Oh...sure, continue to get drunk while your daughter is out there getting ganged raped, fucked and sucked." Gabriella stepped in Yvonna's face. "Don't let this Asian bitch keep you away from your flesh and blood." She said pointing at Ming.

Yvonna was furious. "Don't say that about my little girl again. Ever."

"Are you mad at me?"

"Don't fuck with me," she warned.

"Good!" Gabriella continued clapping her hands together. "Get mad! We can use anger!" She walked behind her on the bed, and placed hands on her shoulder, her lips inches away from her ear. "Because anything you've ever accomplished has been because of how mad you get. I mean look at you now. You're pathetic. Lying on cum crusted floors, getting in cars with strangers and begging for help. You forgot who you are. Haven't you?"

"Yvonna, we don't need her." Ming repeated.

"Sure she does. That's why I'm here. And the sooner she realizes it, the sooner we can get started."

WEDNESDAY

"What you doing?" Aunt Cora asked, standing at the curb after Amanda parked in front of her house.

Amanda smiled but it was out of place. Like a crooked picture in a frame. "I'm going to see Bricks." She moved uneasily. Like the ground was hot.

"Thought you said I could. Because it would keep his spirits raised since —"

"I know what I said."

Raul and four more of her nephews stepped out the house but remained in the yard. It didn't mean that their eyes weren't on her. Amanda was legit scared. "I can go if you want."

"Not until I'm done." She stepped closer. "My boys said they heard you at the door whispering last night in Bricks' room. What were you saying to him?"

"I'm just here to visit." She looked at Raul and his cousins again. "I have no idea what they thought they heard. Maybe a TV was on and —"

Aunt Cora snatched her purse and looked inside. She frowned when she saw a big box of Tampons. "What is this?"

Amanda shrugged. "It's that time of the month."

She handed her purse back. "You got fifteen minutes. Any longer and I'm throwing you out on your ass if I get bad vibes."

On a mental timer, Amanda hustled in the yard, past Raul and his cousins. Once inside, she jumped when she felt them walking closely behind.

Knocking crazily on Bricks' door, she acted as if she were about to pass out. His other cousin sat at a chair texting on his phone.

"When you done knocking you can go inside." He never looked up from his cell.

She looked back at Raul and the others and rushed into Bricks' room. Trembling, she slammed the door. She didn't even notice Bricks had walked up to her because she was filled with so much dread. Taking a deep breath, she wiped a thin mist of sweat from her brow. "Oh my God."

"You got it?" He asked.

"Shhh…" she said looking at the door and back at him. "Yes…but you have to keep your voice down." She walked to the bed and he followed. Flopping down she opened her purse.

He looked inside. "Thanks."

"I'm glad I didn't listen to you and kept them in the box though. You're aunt looked through my purse."

He reached inside, very unsympathetic to her plight or her rattled nerves. "You got a bunch right?"

"Yes, the others are loose under the box. Why you need them?"

He took the box and the extras and shoved them under his bed. "You get the other stuff too?"

She moved apprehensively. He was treating her like a slave. "You know...its rude treating the only person who trying to help you wrong."

He frowned. Pretty or not, this is why he didn't fuck with her from the gate. In his opinion, she was too fickle. "Come on, Amanda. Not this shit again."

"You haven't thanked me once. I mean, what's to stop me from walking out and telling them you're up to something?"

"For starters you don't know what I'm doing."

"I know you're doing something. That's enough for me. It'll be enough for them too. They may even put a chair in here and watch you closer."

He dragged a hand down his face. "First off, I did say thank you."

"You know what." She stood up to leave and he stopped her by shoving her lightly.

"I'm sorry...I just...I gotta get the fuck outta here. I can't lie, I knew my people was capable of some shit like this but...I mean..."

She sat down and touched his hand. "I don't know if I can do what you want, Bricks."

"I just need your help. You all I got. Please?"

"Okay." She smiled.

"When can you get the other stuff?"

"I gotta go to work so in two days I could—"

"Tomorrow." He moved closer. "I need your help tomorrow."

She nodded. "When I come back, I'll have everything you want. But I'ma need you to show how much you appreciate me. You gonna be ready for that?"

CHAPTER TEN
THE PLAN

Yvonna sat in a nail salon getting a full set of stiletto shapes, extra sharp. They were red and it was the first stop of many she had to make if she were going to get Delilah back. And as normal, for the recent days anyway, Ming was on her right and Gabriella on her left.

In a sense, it was as if they represented good versus evil.

When she was finished getting her manicure, she made a stop to the toy store and then the grocers. With a few items in tow, she went to the home of a man she hadn't seen in ages. But she knew despite time, two things would always remain.

Forever.

And they were first, that even if he died, he would see to it that his sons were still running the family business and secondly, that like everyone else in the DMV, they all despised Yvonna Harris.

Nate The Hate vowed like so many others to get revenge if he ever saw her face and so she had to be careful. Still, there was a reason she was there and she

By Reign

had no intentions on leaving until she got what she came for.

When she made it to his neighborhood after catching a ride, she stood on the curb across from the house. To the normal eye, she appeared to be alone, but in her mind Gabriella and Ming hung at her sides, waiting for her next move.

"You know this isn't going to work," Ming said. "If he catches you, he'll kill you."

"The key word is catch," Gabriella said.

Yvonna rubbed her temples. Whenever they bickered it brought her great distress. "Anyway, please...just...just be quiet. I'm trying to think about my next move."

"You can't do what need be done standing over here," Gabriella said. "You gotta get closer." She shoved her forward.

"I'm still not talking to you."

"You aren't talking to anyone remember?" She laughed.

"Shut up!" Yvonna yelled. "Just...just shut up so I can think."

Gabriella rolled her eyes.

Ming crossed her arms over her body.

But Yvonna was focused, wiping her long hair out of her face. When she saw a car pull up in front of Nate's house with a young woman inside, she walked carefully in her direction.

Khloe pulled up, almost bumping the black BMW belonging to Nate The Hate, in front of her. At first she didn't see the vehicle because she was weeping and had to continuously wipe tears away. After backing up some, with the car in park, she pushed around the mounds of junk on her seat to locate her purse.

Grabbing a napkin with the other hand, she blew her nose and wiped her eyes, tossing it back where the rest of the trash rested. Taking a deep breath, she pushed the car door open and the moment she did, her purse fell, emptying its contents in the process.

When she lowered her height to pick up the cosmetics, a wad of money and a separated .22 handgun with a pink handle, she saw Yvonna and jumped. "Who...who are you?"

"What you doing here?"

Khloe opened her mouth and closed it again. Something about Yvonna and the way she stood before her, made her uneasy. "Uh...I am here to see a friend. I'm not—"

"It looks like you dealing guns to me." Yvonna picked up the separated weapon and the money. Next she flashed a fake toy badge and whipped out a Ziploc that she purchased from the grocers before dropping the items inside.

Khloe frowned.

"There's a stakeout at this house." She tried to say it with authority. The thing was, she was too sexy for police. "And if you going inside you'll be arrested."

"Wait...if you a cop, should you be telling me all that?" She frowned.

"Look, I'm doing you a favor. And if you don't get the fuck on, I can take you out of here and down to the precinct." She reached into Khloe's car and grabbed her car keys. "Now scram before I change my mind."

"But you got my keys...how...how can I leave if you won't let me? Give me back my—"

"I'm giving you your freedom instead! You should be grateful."

The girl frowned. Eyes rolling up and down. "I don't believe you a cop."

"I don't care if you—"

Suddenly, the girl yanked Yvonna by her long hair and pulled downward. Yvonna was shocked. She hadn't expected her to fight back. She had soft eyes, the kind that made people take her kindness for a weakness. But it would be the last time Yvonna underestimated someone.

In beast mode, the girl whacked Yvonna on the side of the head, and then the stomach. Yvonna was rusty and did her best to defend herself but it wasn't working. She had to get the kinks out or the girl would continue to get her young life on her face.

Each fighting for the win, the women tussled on the ground until, "Fuck is going on out here?" Nate The Hate said, exiting the house. He was wearing a long blue and gray robe that was worn so much it had small holes throughout.

And he may have been using a cane but the fire in his eyes was still palpable. "I said what the fuck is going on out here?"

"She hit me!" Khloe yelled pointing at her. "You know her?"

From his porch Nate leaned in and squinted. When he saw her face, he glared. "Wait a minute, I know that ain't Yvonna Harris on the curb of my fucking house! I heard she was crazy but she had to have really lost her mind if she here. When she know I'm looking for that head!"

"Yvonna Harris," each of his three nephews repeated as they exited the house. Each stronger and more muscular than the man before him.

"She say she police!" Khloe yelled, wiping her hair out of her face. "She trying to take my car too!"

"That bitch ain't no police!" Nate yelled. "She the devil himself." He looked at his youngins. "Get her and bring her to me with her neck cracked like an egg! That bitch got a price on her head! And I wanna get paid for it! "

"I knew you weren't a cop!" Khloe yelled.

Yvonna quickly grabbed the keys off the ground, which had fallen due to the scuffle. Hitting it to the car, she was immediately weighed down when Khloe jumped on her back. Yvonna's legs gave out and they both fell to the ground just before the nephews made it out the yard.

But Yvonna was relentless and shook her off quickly, making it to the car and peeling away from the scene, just before Nate The Hate's goons tried to get a hold of her.

Yvonna got away, the trouble was, Khloe was in the back seat.

"What you doing here? Get out!"

"What is your problem?" Khloe yelled easing to the front passenger seat. "What do you want with me?"

"Your car a garbage dump and you asking me what's wrong?"

"Like you said, this my car! I can do with it how I please."

"Ming starting to think you like trouble," Ming said from the backseat. "You supposed to be looking for Delilah and you pick up a stray?"

"Trouble is the foreplay of sex," Gabriella interjected. "Let the woman be."

"Leave me alone!" Yvonna looked at them from the rearview mirror. "Both of you."

Khloe looked in the back seat and back at Yvonna. She didn't see a thing. "What...who are you talking to?"

"You know I could hurt you right?" Yvonna looked dead into Khloe's eyes. "I'm the wrong person to be near these days. Didn't you hear Nate?"

She had.

She pulled a deep breath. He did seem like she was all types of evil but she was determined to fight for her car. "Yeah, I can tell by how Nate looked at you something's wrong but I can't...I can't..." She broke down crying. "You can't have my car. I'm sorry."

"Get rid of this bitch," Gabriella said.

"Earlier today, I was supposed to be going on vacation with my fiancé. We paid for it and everything." She wiped tears away. "I was at work on my way to the airport and he told me he couldn't go. Said his co-worker who was supposed to take over his shift got sick. So his boss called him in and our vacation was cut. Said if he didn't, he wouldn't have a job when he came back."

"She's annoying as fuck," Gabriella said.

"I was gonna go by myself at first." Khloe continued. "Didn't want to waste the money but I didn't wanna go without him either."

"Listen, I got a lot on my plate and this...whatever it is...ain't me."

"If you stealing my car, the least you can do is listen to me." She sniffled. "I mean can you be actually that heartless?"

Yes. She could.

"Yvonna, you can be a little kinder." Ming said. "She may have something to tell you of importance. So relax." She shrugged. "It's just Ming's opinion. I—"

"Since when have you been this soft?" Yvonna responded.

"Maybe you feel the need to make her that way." Gabriella interjected. "Good, verses evil. Never forget, we're here because of you."

"You're starting to scare me." Khloe said, looking behind her and back at Yvonna. "Are you okay?"

"What you want with me?" Yvonna asked glaring. "I'm not your fucking friend."

"Like I said, I need somebody to…to listen. Can you do that for me? At least?"

"Awe," Ming said.

"Hurry up," Yvonna responded.

She sniffled and wiped her tears and nose. "Okay, so, so, I get back home, and my dog is yelping before I even get inside."

"Dogs yelp all the time."

"But he's blind," she sniffled. "He only yelps when one person is around. My sister Fiona. He never barks or whimpers except with her. I think she kicks him and he can't stand her. He can smell her ass."

Yvonna shrugged. "So your sister was there."

"Don't you see, my *sister* was in my house." She placed her hand over her heart. "Me and my fiancé were supposed to be out of town and he all of a sudden didn't want to go. So my fiancé and my sister were together. And when they saw my car, to get my dog to stop barking, they...they tossed him out the window." She reached in the back on the floor and snatched a sheet off a mound next to all the junk. Hidden beneath was a dead brown Yorkie.

Upon seeing the carcass, Yvonna quickly pulled over. "What the fuck? You have a dead dog in here?"

"So I went inside the house, demanding that they come out but they wouldn't open the bedroom door." Khloe continued quickly as if time were running out. "So, so I went to the kitchen to get my gun, the one I bought from Nate last week but it came apart. He sold me a gun that fell apart! Can you believe that shit?"

"I'm five seconds from going off on you! Hurry up and get to the point, bitch."

"Okay, okay, I need a gun that works so I can kill my sister and fiancé for betraying me. So, so they can never hurt me again. Ever."

"So you want revenge?"

She nodded rapidly, tears rolling down her chin. "You have no idea how it feels to be betrayed."

"Trust me, you don't want revenge. You want to get your things and leave your sister and fiancé be. I promise it's for the best."

CLICK.

When Khloe heard the sound and looked downward, she saw her gun aimed in her direction. Yvonna had put it together without her knowing. "It wasn't broken. It was taken apart, probably by your fiancé. To prevent you from using it. People do it all the time when cleaning."

"I don't understand. It was in two pieces. I—."

"Get out."

She didn't move.

"Now."

Slowly Khloe backed out the car slamming the door behind herself.

Yvonna sped off.

Standing in the bathroom mirror, Yvonna looked at her reflection. Nate The Hate sending his relations to kill her reverberated what she already knew. That the city, America even, wanted her annihilated.

But America could kiss her ass.

She wasn't going anywhere.

If she were going to survive, she needed to resort to her old ways, even if she knew it would bring her more pain later. But for her little girl, she would do anything.

Picking up the scissors off the sink, she grabbed a lump of hair and clipped. Moving to the other side she clipped again until her hair was blunt, a little on the top and barely any on the sides.

Afterwards, she washed her hair and smoothed down the edges, leaving the top short and spiky.

Gabriella appeared behind her and smiled. "There go my bitch." She paused. "What took you so fucking long?"

CHAPTER ELEVEN
THURSDAY

Bricks walked out of his room and into the hallway, the moment he did, his aunt strolled up to him. "Thanks for this," she grabbed his face with both hands and looked inside the room. Sunlight slid through an open window, turning the urine inside of the jars on his floor the color of honey.

"No problem."

She dropped her hands. Disgusted. "I know you didn't want to have breakfast with the family but it means a lot to me." She looked at the jars again and frowned.

"You kept me in prison, so I acted like I was in prison."

"I never wanted you cooped up in your room, Marlon." He hated when she called him by his middle name. "Going to the bathroom was always an option. You just never took it." She touched his face again as Raul stepped next to her. "Now, let us act more like family and not fight."

He looked at his cousin and then his aunt. Taking a deep breath he said, "Something smells good. What you cooking?"

"Nothing but all your favorites."

He rubbed his belly and shrugged. "Then let's eat."

The Mean Receptionist was just about to enjoy her sour cream donut when Yvonna walked inside and wedged a stopper under the door to prevent it from opening from the outside. The Mean Receptionist felt she looked familiar but with the short spiked hair, along with the dark makeup, she could no longer place her face. Everything about her seemed different because everything about her *was* different.

Yvonna moved slowly toward the counter and leaned on it. She was cool as recently melted ice.

"Can…can I help you?" She asked, although she never really wanted to help a soul.

"Remember me?"

Her voice sent chills down her spine. "Uh…I don't know what this is about but the doctor can't see you right now."

"I know. No one is here except you and I."

Yvonna scanned her surroundings and when she saw what she wanted, she walked through the door, behind the counter and up to a dookie brown leather purse.

"Excuse me!" The Mean Receptionist yelled. "You can't be back here and you can't be touching my things."

Yvonna treated her as if she wasn't there. Instead, she raised the purse, dug inside and searched for her wallet. Grabbing her driver's license, she took a picture and tossed the license in her face. The document nicked her nose.

When the Mean Receptionist jumped up, Yvonna pushed her back and dragged her sharp stiletto shaped nails across her cheek. They were so pointed that it was as if five sharp knives were slicing into her skin.

In shock and fear, the Mean Receptionist held the wounds as blood poured beneath them like a weak water fountain.

Yvonna lowered her height and smiled. "Now, now, don't be afraid."

"What do you want?" She whispered.

"First let me tell you what I know already." She stood up. "I know where you live. And you should understand that I have nothing to lose. What I don't know are the names of the people who were here the day my daughter went missing. But you will help me with that." She slashed the other side of her face just for fun and the woman cried.

"Please stop."

"Bitch, the way you treated me, you should be glad I'm not killing your ass." She sighed. "So, you will tell me the names of each and every patient who was here the day Delilah Harris came. And you will keep the information you tell me private. Because if you don't, I will go into hiding, only coming out to make your life a living hell. And then, when you beg for mercy, I will kill you."

The men were all seated in the living room when Cinnamon finally ascended the steps from the basement, where a group of eight waited. A small smile stretched across his face and he looked proud of himself and arrogant all at once. "She's sleep," he said, closing the door.

"I get all that but where the fuck is Yvonna?" Alex snapped. The child's well-being was of no concern if she didn't bring him closer to his enemy.

Cinnamon's face melted like butter in a hot cast iron pan. "She's not telling me where they staying."

Alex frowned and looked back at the men and then Cinnamon. "When we came for yet another meeting you promised we would be drinking her blood before the night ended."

"And you will."

"Which night though?" He yelled. "When I find her myself? Because I gotta tell you, right now, you not looking like a man of your word."

"He's gonna find her," Silva told Alex. "Just trust him."

"Nigga, ain't nobody trying to hear all that shit."

"Be easy." Cinnamon warned pointing at Alex.

"Or what?" Alex's wife, Brittany asked.

"Babe, don't."

"Nah, he claimed he always had eyes on her. And that you would finally get justice. Now my husband hung his life on that fact because he loved Dave."

"We all did," Cinnamon responded.

"But you were the one who promised us Yvonna. Not me." Alex continued. "And now all we have is a girl."

"Nobody wants her head to roll more than me." He pointed at himself, before bringing a boulder-sized fist down over his chest. "And I still gotta wait too. But I promise you this, it won't be for long."

"Nate The Hate said she stopped by his house. Still on her crazy shit too. Without a care in the world. The way it look she don't give a fuck about the hunt or that little bitch downstairs."

Cinnamon glared. "What she go there for?"

"He don't know. But he thinks it was to rob his customers before they got into his house. Nate ain't changed shit in over twenty years. Every nigga with a bill know he operates a cash only business."

"Every nigga with a bill also know robbing him is suicide too."

"But we talking about Yvonna Harris. She already dead." Alex shook his head. "And anyway she got away."

Cinnamon smiled. "You see...he has niggas on the ready and not one could grab her."

"I don't give a fuck!" Alex yelled louder. "She killed Dave! And we owe him. All of us. That bitch must die."

"And she will. Now we have who she wants. Sit back and let her come to us."

This was not the hood but its cousin.

Still, the bustling restaurant was busy as Yvonna stepped inside. Her body still on point, she gained the attention of every patron present. Her physique was cold. Wearing tight jeans, a fitted white t-shirt and red high heels, she finally felt uniformed enough to do her job.

And per usual, Gabriella and Ming were at her sides.

"Can I help you," a male host asked, catching each of her curves as if he were a surfer. "With anything at all?"

She grinned, eyes hidden behind dark shades. "Um, yes, actually. I'm looking for my cousin."

"Okay, who dat?"

"The owner. Courtney Smite."

He frowned. "Oh, I'm sorry. I...I didn't know you were the boss's family. Please don't tell her I was coming onto you. I was just—."

"Where is she?"

He swallowed hard. "In the kitchen." He pointed behind himself. "In her office I think."

She shoved him to the side with the back of her hand and entered the kitchen without an invite. Once in the back, the sound of onions and green peppers being sliced on cut boards permeated the air. Since there were four women, all dressed in white chef jackets, Yvonna didn't know who she was.

"Courtney!" She yelled.

A cute red bone with light brown hair turned around. And as if she knew her, she waved for her to follow her to the back.

"What's up with this crazy bitch?" Yvonna asked. Her gesture seemed awkward since they never met a day in their lives.

"Yeah, you should talk," Gabriella responded.

A minute later, they were in Courtney's office. It was a small space that was crowded to the guild with colorful books on recipes. "I thought they were

sending a guy." She sat in a chair that rocked happily. "I must admit, this is way smarter."

Her name was on the list the Mean Receptionist provided. And she was there to question the woman about what her daughter might have seen the day Delilah was taken. So what was she talking about now?

"I'm here about your daughter," Yvonna said.

"I know." She yanked the drawer and pulled out a safe. Opening it, she handed her an address and a stack of money. Next she removed a picture and stared at it for many moments before giving it to Yvonna.

The photo was of a handsome man with hazel eyes, the color of her light brown hair. He was wearing a white shirt with burnt orange flowers scattered about and a lei rested around his neck.

Placing the photo down, Yvonna thumbed through the money. It was over three thousand dollars easy. Coupled with what she got from Khloe, she was up thirty five hundred.

"I'll give you the rest when the job is done."

"Tell her you aren't who she thinks." Ming said. "You here for Delilah. Stay focused."

Yvonna rubbed her forehead briskly, doing her best not to answer, which would immediately alert Courtney that she was weird. Yes she knew they weren't there, but they felt as real to her as a hand to the small of a back. A kiss on the cheek. A slap to the face.

"You need that money," Gabriella responded. "Don't be stupid. You can't give it back."

Yvonna rubbed her head harder causing the chef to frown. "Are you...are you okay? I have some aspirin if—."

"What you want done?" Yvonna pointed down at the picture.

Courtney adjusted a little in her seat. "I explained to Huff already. I don't want to know."

"You're paying for this...surely you have some idea of what you're seeking."

Courtney nodded and smiled. "Running over the nigga would get me right."

"Oh my goodness, finally some action," Gabriella grinned, rubbing her hands together as if trying to start a fire.

Yvonna crossed her legs and sat back comfortably. "What did he do?"

She sighed deeply, as if sucking the air from the room. "We have joint custody of our sixteen-year-old daughter. After our separation two years ago. And Lisa, well, she isn't the easiest person to deal with. But it's mainly because she doesn't have a firm grasp on reality, which is why she's seeing a doctor. It's been that way all her life." Her head dropped. "You have no idea what it takes to deal with a mentally ill child."

She was wrong.

She was speaking to the Queen of Crazy herself.

"Recently I learned he'd been self medicating her for years. If that's what you want to call it. Technically I call it child alcohol abuse."

"I don't understand."

"He was putting Hennessy and sleeping pills inside of ice tea. So he could...just so he could have his whore every night, without the benefit of our daughter's rants because she would be sleep." She glared. "He actually calls her a brat. Says she's begging for attention. But she loves that man so much she's starting to hate me. So I need him gone."

"She still loves him," Ming said.

"And I want him to pay!" Courtney continued.

"We don't have time for this!" Ming repeated.

Yvonna sat forward. "I want to ask you about something. On the day she last went to the doctor did she see anything crazy?"

She frowned. "I don't know. Why?"

"You digging holes." Gabriella responded. "Let's take the money and bounce."

"Think!"

Courtney jumped. "I can't remember. All I know is she went drinking with her friends again and it was because of him. Had he not been giving her alcohol she wouldn't have had a problem."

The door opened. It was the male host who found Yvonna tantalizing. "There's a man here to see you."

"Tell him to wait." Courtney said.

"Let's go," Gabriella whispered. "I think it's the man who's job you're about to take."

"Ming smell danger too." Ming added.

"Were you there?" Yvonna asked Courtney, trying to keep focus. "The day she was at the appointment. To see the doctor?" Yvonna couldn't remember.

"What you want me to tell him?" The Male Host interrupted. "He said his name is —."

"Get the fuck out!" Yvonna yelled at him. "Now!"

"I was there."

He looked at his boss and then Yvonna before running away, closing the door behind himself.

"Did you see anything?" Yvonna asked harsher. "Anything at all? I don't care how small."

She frowned. "No."

"Let's go." Ming begged looking at the door.

"I'm with the Asian now." Gabriella replied. "Don't make me take over your body to get us out of here."

"Don't threaten me." Yvonna responded, letting her crazy out the bag. But accepting the threat, she rose and moved toward the door.

"I'm not threatening you," the woman said. "What about my daughter?"

Yvonna looked at her once more and walked out.

Courtney followed just as they passed the Male Host and the man who was trying to get in to meet her.

"Who are you?" Courtney asked the man as Yvonna quickly ran towards the door.

"Huff sent me. For the job."

Courtney rotated her head quickly to Yvonna who was almost out the door. "Stop her! Now!"

Parked outside, Yvonna sat in her stolen car across from the man in the photo Courtney had given her. He was placing several fold-up chairs in the hatch of his black truck, totally unaware of the killer in his midst.

"What we doing here?" Ming asked.

Gabriella grinned sinisterly. "You know what we 'bout to do. Shut up, girl."

Yvonna knew she didn't have to do the task for the money she took, but she did feel out of contact with who she used to be. Maybe quickly ending a man who deserved it would rejuvenate her a little.

With that in mind, she pressed her foot on the gas pedal and rolled him over, killing him instantly.

CHAPTER TWELVE

It was dark.

So why was he outside?

Alone?

Jordan sat in his yard, in a red lawn chair, looking into the darkness. About fifteen-years-old, he looked troubled. Gray circles around the eyes. Wrinkles on the forehead. He was wearing the face of a man almost twenty years his senior. When Yvonna walked down the block, only his eyes moved to greet her.

She wasn't hopeful that he would have any information. But he was the final person on her list, after having gone to everyone else, he was truly her last chance. The way she saw it was simple. Someone witnessed Delilah being taken. She just had to find out whom.

The thing was, her day had already been long.

The second person she went to see after Courtney, was a little girl. She was ten-years-old and when Yvonna knocked on the door to ask if the child or her mother remembered anything strange the day Delilah was taken, the door was slammed in her face.

Later in the day, the woman realized Yvonna would not be deterred when she was at the park, sitting on a bench breast-feeding her child, while the other played. Not fucking around, Yvonna walked up, and choked her from behind.

"Call her over here," Yvonna said, looking at the girl who was at the doctor's office that day. The girl was on a swing even though she looked like she was large enough to be playing football for the "U" in Miami.

"Elena, come over here!" The mother said, as the baby in her arms wailed. "My...my friend wants to ask you something."

Elena walked toward them. "Yes...yes, mom?" Her eyes stayed on Yvonna even though she was talking to her mother. After awhile, and a line of serious questioning, it was obvious that she hadn't seen anything, so Yvonna was set back again.

The third person she visited was a fifteen-year-old boy and his mother. The moment Yvonna knocked on the door she was invited in quickly. The mother, a large white woman with sores on her legs, went on and on about her favorite TV shows as her son sat at her side, looking at Yvonna, embarrassed into space. When she wasn't talking about her shows she went on about her neighbors, and how everyone was jealous of the life she built for her son as a single mother.

She even bragged about her car, a used white paint chipped Mercedes that sat in the driveway. She bragged about the new furniture she bought last week with the cigarette holes in them and she bragged about all the homemade meals she made for her son in a kitchen so rancid it was hard to breathe, even as Yvonna sat in the living room, holding her breath.

At the end of the day Yvonna left feeling badly for the son because one thing was obvious. It was she who needed mental health care, not him.

And of course, they provided zero information.

She placed her hands on the fence. "You're Jordan right?" She moved closer but wanted to be careful. Something about his eyes told her that he was different.

"Bees are dying. And nobody cares. Like what are we gonna do when they gone?"

Yvonna looked at the opened fence. "Can I come in? It's just that, I want to talk to you about a few things if you don't mind."

"I don't think we care enough," he continued. "About anything? Do you?"

"I care about stuff."

He leveled a dark gaze. "I don't believe you."

"You were in the psychiatrist's office, about three days ago. Did you see anything that looks — "

"They took her." His gaze fell down. "I tried to tell people but no one cared. Why don't people care?"

"He knows something." Gabriella said standing behind her. "Catch him."

She was right. Yvonna's heart kicked up speed. She rushed inside the gate, just as he moved around back. He wasn't running but he was quick, with the gait of a professional runner.

And the path he took looked grim and it caused her senses to heighten. Although she was outside, it looked as if the boy disappeared into the mouth of a beast.

Her mind told her to run back to the car but she was not going to let him get away until he told her what he'd seen. And so she followed him, through the wild hanging brush that scratched against her face as she crept toward the backyard.

When she made it around back, she was startled at first at figures within the darkness. Taking a deeper look, she relaxed when she realized it was only furniture. The pieces were propped on top of one another as if someone wanted easy access to the grass below.

The thing was, in the black of night they looked like men.

And then there was the open door, with the light on. What was going on inside the house?

Every fiber of her being knew things were dangerous but by the time she realized she should be fearful, she was already inside.

Once in the kitchen, she walked up on a table, with four muscular white men sitting around it. Their frames covered with tattoos, a few of the designs racist. They were in serious conversation, that Yvonna interrupted and their eyes brewed with fire.

"I got a feeling they gonna hate your black ass." Gabriella said stating the obvious. "Maybe this wasn't smart after all."

Jordan stood behind the man at the furthest end of the table. It was at that time she could tell that Jordan was possibly mixed and that these men could be of some relation.

"I'm sorry to interrupt but I need him to answer a few questions." She pointed at the boy. "And I'm not leaving until he does just that."

"Who are you?" Asked the one closest to Jordan. He rose.

She took one step back, toward the open doorway. "I don't mean anyone any harm. I just…well…your son —"

"My nephew." He corrected her.

He stepped from around the table. Closer. And she could see a gun in his waistband. As a matter of fact, when she looked around it was obvious they were all packing. She also noticed money stacks on the table.

Was she interrupting a drug deal?

"Listen, I don't want any trouble. And I don't care about whatever is going on here. I just —."

Suddenly she felt a searing pain rip through her arm right before she felt a warm syrup like sensation running down her wrist. It was her blood. Quickly she took an about-face just as another bullet went flying over her shoulder blade.

Scared for what was left of her life, she swore she could feel the earth spinning, and as a result was light footed and delirious. She ran quickly, branches and thick grass growing under her feet. From where she was she could see the car but it seemed so far away. But when she turned around she was being hunted.

At the end of the day all Yvonna got for her troubles were more enemies.

What a waste of time.

Yvonna was driving slowly down the street after taking a bullet to the arm. She realized that the stolen car she was in could not be used any longer. She had plans to abandon it later.

But now was the time.

In total pain, she parked in an open garage some ways up from her next destination. Then she got out, holding her arm while running up the street.

"Hey, you can't leave this here!" A man yelled. "Excuse me! You can't leave this car here!"

CHAPTER THIRTEEN

The rain poured heavily.

The electricity had gone out earlier but came back on with flickers every fifteen minutes. Afraid a future power outage may be permanent; Aunt Cora demanded everyone turn out all lights, with the exception of television sets. Bricks wasn't interested in watching anything.

So he remained in the dark.

His mind was still on his plan.

He had been smoothing things out with his aunt, but it was all a part of his scheme. To get back to Yvonna. It was also obvious it wasn't going to be easy. Raul was still guarding him closely and so he spent most of the time in his room. Away from his gaze.

Bricks was sitting on the edge of the bed looking out of the window when there was a knock at the door. "Come in," he said, without looking to see who entered.

"Hey." Amanda said, locking the door. "I thought you would be sleep by now."

"Nah." He continued to look at the rain pouring outside. "You got the stuff?"

allowed him to slip and slide right into an orgasm that he splashed on her back.

When they were done, he got dressed and looked over at her when she was still lying down. "Get up, Amanda. We gotta get to work."

"Wow...not gonna hold me or nothing?" She grabbed her panties and slid them over her soggy pussy. Old girl thought they were going to fuck all night.

"Either get up or get the fuck out. Your call."

The living room was completely dim. Amanda was sitting on the sofa with Raul. He was watching television and from his position, he could see Bricks' door.

When the movie was thirty minutes in, she pulled out a bottle of Wild Irish Rose and one of the four small plastic cups in her purse. Pouring the drink into one, his eyes rolled toward the bottle and then quickly back onto the television.

He was nervous.

"What you doing?" He asked, never removing his gaze from the set.

"I'm thirsty." She sipped all of the liquor and drank another. When she had her fill, she stuffed the bottle and used cup back in her purse. "Why?"

Silence.

"This movie so good." She continued. "I should've watched it awhile ago." She shrugged. "Don't know why I haven't."

Whenever she spoke, he could smell the sweet scent of the liquor and it made his stomach flip, like a first kiss. If only he could have one taste he would be good. Was this Bricks' plan? He felt a set up coming and had no intentions on playing the victim. Besides, he hadn't drank in over ten years.

"What you doing?" He asked, eyes still on the TV although he had no idea what was happening. He wanted a taste so bad, the people resembled blobs and their forms meshed into the background.

"What you mean?" When she spoke again, the scent of liquor kissed the air once more.

"I haven't touched the stuff in years and I'm not about to start now. So tell Bricks he can suck my dick."

"Raul, you act like I haven't always come over here and watched TV with you, even before Bricks came back. I don't know what you talking about."

"Yeah right, everybody knows the only reason you came over was to find out what was up with Bricks."

She shrugged. "That may be true but I'm still just chilling." With each word the liquor seemed to gas the air, making him weak. She moved to get up. "I mean, if you want me to leave then—"

"No." He said holding her wrist firmly. As if she were under arrest. "Just...just stay."

Got him. She thought.

She took her seat, dug into her purse and removed the bottle, except this time she released two cups. "You drinking or what? I mean, after ten years I would say you not an alcoholic no more. Wouldn't you? Prove you have self-control. Enjoy a drink with me."

She had a point to hear him think it.

His cousins drank all the time. Although normally they would sip on beer and vodka, none of which he liked. But the Wild Irish Rose was his daddy's drink and it hit different. It was almost as if taking a sip would transport him back to the days when they shared a cup.

Before the law got a hold of him and his father was murdered.

Fifteen minutes later, he had tossed his cup and consumed the entire bottle. Since the bottle was mixed with a few Benny's, courtesy of Bricks and Amanda, he was nauseous and sleepy immediately.

When his stomach swirled even more, he rushed to the bathroom and threw up in the toilet. Although he hadn't consumed liquor in years, he was surprised at how badly he handled it. When he was done throwing up his guts, he stumbled in the living room where she was still seated on the sofa. "Get out!" He wiped his mouth with the back of his hand.

"What I do?"

He stomped toward her and grabbed her by the arm. Digging into his pocket he removed the key that locked from the inside. Unlocking the door, he tossed her out with a shove to the upper back, stuffed the key in his pocket and fell face down on the sofa.

Five minutes later, Bricks came out of his room. When he saw Raul sleep, first he crept into the kitchen. Next he reached into his pocket and grabbed a hand full of tampons. One by one he stuffed them in the faucet tightly before creeping by Raul who was still sleep.

Now in the bathroom, he filled the faucets and the tub with tampons until it was packed thick and no water exited. Once done, he grabbed a handful more and flushed them down the toilet repeatedly. When he walked out, Raul was sitting on the sofa, head down, hands clasped in front of him like a disappointed father.

"I know what you did." His head slowly rose as he looked directly at his cousin. "And that shit hurts too."

Bricks crossed his arms. "What you talking about?"

Thunder clapped outside. The lights flickered.

"You knew I was sober and you went through all this shit, just to get at a bitch who gonna get you killed." He shook his head and flopped face up on the sofa. "The thing is I still love you and you not leaving this house."

"Come on, man. Ain't nobody trying to—."

"But you forgot one thing." He dug into his pocket and removed the key. "I got this and you still not getting out. Every door and window in this house is locked. Now get the fuck up out my face, inmate."

CHAPTER FOURTEEN

Stitched up, Yvonna walked back into her motel room.

She couldn't believe how a simple act of questioning those in the waiting room the day Delilah was taken, could end in her being shot. And at the same time, she had taken a man's life for sport that week, so she figured as always the Universe rewarded her in kind.

It was called karma.

When she made it to her room, she tossed the key on the floor and gently flopped face up in the bed. She called Bricks' cell phone many times and was still unsuccessful in reaching him. Although she was more focused on doing what was necessary, and not allowing her emotions to rule the day, not talking to Bricks hit different.

She knew his family despised her but she was hoping that he would try harder to help her.

It was breaking her heart that he was not.

After being unsuccessful with reaching Bricks, she took a deep breath and dialed the one number of a man she knew held the keys to helping her.

Jabar.

Sure she went to him earlier in the week. But she felt confident that if she tried harder, he would relent. Besides, they had twin personalities.

They both were mentally ill. In fact, when they were connected in the past, Jabar's bipolar episodes put her in an emotional tug of war because when it was good, it was great, but when it was bad she was left feeling alone. Wondering what she could do to save their bond. He was mentally draining, just like her, but he was loyal.

His mood swings were also why he was never *the one*.

After calling a few numbers trying to reach him and getting the run around, she lucked up on a child who answered the phone. This same child willingly told her, her uncle's number, and that was all she needed.

He answered on the first ring. "Who dis?"

"Jabar…it's…its me again."

He let out a long breath that she could almost feel. "Nah…I…I can't fuck with you. I told you that already. Why you keep hitting me? And how you get my number?"

"Jabar, please, I don't have nobody. Please don't do this to me. I need you."

Silence.

"Jabar? You there?"

"My number gonna be changed by morning." He hung up.

"Fuck!" She yelled as she ran her hands down her face.

"Are you ready to hear what I have to say yet?" Gabriella asked. "Because, I won't lend my advice unless — ."

"I have things under control." She was lying.

"Sure you do," she smiled sitting down. "You just gave five hundred dollars to a nurse who removed a bullet and stitched you up at urgent care. And you also left before the cops came to question you about how you got the wound. So yeah, you doing a great job ain't you?"

Yvonna winced a little in pain. "Just a set back that's all."

"If you say so."

"I know Jordan knows something, and he's going to tell me." She stood up and walked toward the bathroom. "Whether he wants to or not."

"Sure he will. You just have to get past the five white killers who at your neck." She laughed. "They probably think you were trying to take the pack. Or rob them."

"The whole world is after me." She shrugged and wiped her face with cool water. "They can get in line with everyone else."

"If you ask me, your time is almost up. I mean, can't you feel it? It's that feeling in your stomach when you're about to cum, instead you're pushed off a building."

She did feel it, but ignored the sensation.

Yvonna placed both hands on the cool sink and observed herself in the mirror. "Where's Ming?"

"If you don't see her, it means you're tiring of the good part in your mind." She laid her head on Yvonna's shoulder. "Maybe you officially gone to the darker side. With me."

MOMENTS EARLIER

Yvonna made a mistake as she walked into the motel that night. She didn't see the nigga in a white pick up truck who had just left Zyla's room. He was picking up a few bundles of hair for his nine-month pregnant girlfriend who wanted to look good on the Gram when she went into labor the next day.

As he watched Yvonna walk in her room, he fumbled with his phone until he dialed the number he was trying to reach. "Aye, nigga! You won't believe this shit."

"What is it?"

"I got eyes on Yvonna Harris!"

Cinnamon hung up the phone on the kitchen wall and stormed into the living room, up to the rest of the killers. They had been going over possible situations to let the city know they had Delilah, hoping to draw Yvonna out of her hole.

But the news he held was better.

"You won't believe this shit." Cinnamon said with a grin. His wife eased against his side as he held her tightly.

"What is it, babe?"

He smiled down at her and looked at his men. "I know where she is."

Every man in the room rose from his seat. "Don't play with me like this," Alex said. "I can't take it."

"I know where she at," he repeated. "It's time to go get that bitch."

Alex frowned. "What happened to letting her come to us?"

"Never look a gift horse in the mouth." He pointed at him. "She don't even know eyes on her. We got her right where we want her. Its like taking candy from a crazy."

CHAPTER FIFTEEN

B ricks opened his eyes slowly and when he did, he saw water seeping under his bedroom door. Smiling, he quickly got dressed, slipped into his shoes and waited. Within seconds, there was a bang on the door followed by his Aunt Cora entering in panic mode.

Behind her, in the living room, he could see his cousins running back and forth with buckets and cups, trying to scoop water off the floor and out of the house.

"Bricks, I need you to help," she said in a shaky voice. "It's bad. Real bad."

He rubbed his eyes. "What's, what's wrong though?"

"I don't know. The water wasn't coming out full flow and then the pipes exploded in the walls and the toilet overflowed. Shit is everywhere."

"So, what you want me to do?"

"Grab some towels and help soak it up." She cried before she could finish. "Oh, Bricks, I can't lose my house. I just can't." She sniffled again.

"You think scooping up water gonna work? You may need to get some help."

"Raul going to rent a few dehumidifiers until the plumbers come. This...this has worked my nerves." She cried hard and Bricks felt extreme guilt. At the same time, she brought this on herself, trying to keep man from wife. "I'm so scared."

He gripped her shoulders. "You won't lose your house, Aunt Cora. Trust me. You just have to stay focused."

She nodded and they walked out of his room. Not trusting him, the rest of his cousins looked at him and shook their heads. For a moment Bricks wondered if they knew he was responsible.

But he could care less.

All he wanted was to get out find Yvonna and make sure she was good. He also wanted to slide past his Aunt Shonda's house since she was taking care of Chomps per a Child Protective Services order. Although they talked, he hadn't seen him and he missed the kid.

Aunt Cora had confiscated his phone earlier that week so he couldn't even do face time. He had to go primitive and talk on the phone sitting on the kitchen wall. It wasn't the same; he needed to see the boy's face.

On the other hand, part of him was relieved she had him. Chomps was a loose string and he didn't need him in the midst of the fire.

Keeping up with the scheme, he dropped to hands and knees, and helped his family soak up water due to a well-executed plan.

And the door was wide open.

Yvonna stuffed her cell phone back under her pillow, something she did often, after checking it only to see zero calls or messages.

Sitting on the edge of the bed she tried to clean up the bandaged bullet wound which began to bleed a little.

"You want to hear what I think now?" Gabriella said.

"You know what, I prefer Ming." She wiped the wound again with pieces of rough tissue. "At least she's more positive."

"If that were true, why isn't she here?"

"Leave me alone."

"You in over your head and there's one reason and one reason only."

Yvonna sighed. "And what's that?"

"You still refuse to embrace who you are." She eased closer. "Sure you killed the one man this year. But it's like you a teenager all over again. Scared. Milk on the breath. Hogging the use of your body, and not allowing me to take over. We both know I'm the most dominant and responsible of us all. With me in control, we get shit done."

"This my body and I decide who's in charge! Leave me the fuck alone!" Yvonna screamed.

RING! RING! RING!

"Now look what you did. Somebody probably calling to complain." She picked up the phone. "Who is this?"

"It's Zyla. You—"

CLICK.

Yvonna hung up because there was no way she was going to waste time talking to a person she didn't know or like. The only reason she answered was because she didn't know if Delilah or Bricks would reach out.

KNOCK! KNOCK! KNOCK! BANG! BANG! BANG!

"I'll give her one thing, she's a persistent little bitch." Gabriella grinned, looking at the door.

Reapplying the tape quickly on her arm, she hopped up and opened the door with an attitude. This time she would kick her ass.

That was on mothers.

The moment the door widened, she was snatched out and a hand was slammed over her mouth. Within seconds, she was taken in another room where the lights were all out and the curtains were drawn, making the room crayon black.

Only the sound of her own breath could be heard.

And still, she knew she wasn't alone.

"I can't take my hand off your mouth right now," a man with a deep voice whispered. "I'm sorry."

Yvonna struggled but it was of no use, he was stronger. Since she wasn't hurt at the moment, she decided to patiently wait and save her energy.

Five minutes passed and suddenly she heard a door crash outside the room, followed by the soft whisper of anxious voices. When she looked under the doorway, where the light from the outside shined through, she could see several sets of feet scurrying back and forth.

"Be easy," the man who was holding her mouth said to her. "Be real easy and don't make a sound."

"Where the fuck is she then?" A man said to another outside the room.

"You think I fucking know?" Another responded.

"Fuck! We had that bitch right where we wanted and now look. She got away again!"

"At least we got her daughter," one man said.

Hearing that Delilah was in their possession, Yvonna wiggled to her heart's content, trying to get free, but the man would not release his hold. He seemed dead set on keeping her under his grasp. And suddenly...KNOCK! BANG! KNOCK!

One of the angry men outside obviously wanted the attention of the neighbor next door. Where Yvonna was hidden. Instead of being afraid, Yvonna wanted to sacrifice herself, but the man pressed down on her lips harder, almost to the point of stopping her breath.

After thirty more seconds in silence the man on the other side said, *"If I find out you have her, whoever you are, I will be back. And I will kill you."* He promised. *"She's not worth it. Let us have her."*

Us? They all thought.

Eventually, the man walked away.

After ten more minutes in darkness, one light from the bathroom within the motel room was turned on. It was at that time that Yvonna saw Zyla, Marge and two men.

"Fuck did you do that for?" She yelled shoving the large man. He bopped backwards but remained on his feet.

"I told him to do it." Zyla responded.

"Fuck for?!"

"Because I been running a successful business out this motel for years," she paused. "And one more murder and this place will be shut down. And I can't let your dead ass fuck it up."

"But they have my daughter!" Yvonna yelled pointing at the door. "I could've given myself up and —."

"What? Die?" Zyla yelled. "It's clear they want your head! And giving up yourself for your daughter won't stop them."

"She's right," Marge said. "If anything they'll kill you both."

"How did you know?" Yvonna asked.

"One of my customers told me. He a messy nigga who came for a few packs. Thought it was funny."

"I really think you should hear what I have to say," Gabriella whispered in her ear. "I have an idea."

"Leave me alone!" Yvonna yelled.

"And I'll do all that," Zyla responded, not knowing she was talking to one of the many voices that occupied her mind. "But not on this property. Not while I'm doing business."

Devastated, Yvonna shoved several bundles of hair to the floor and plopped on the bed. Although she hated to admit it, she knew Zyla was right. "I can't believe this shit."

"Who are those people?" Zyla asked.

"Just one of the many niggas wanting to kill me."

Zyla laughed. "Now *that* I can believe."

"This ain't funny."

"Never said it was. Just stating the facts."

"They may be back." Yvonna warned. "I have some things in my room and I'm gonna need somebody to fix the door. I won't be able to check out until my daughter returns. She knows I'm there. That room is our only connection."

"We have the door under control," Marge said. "It will be fixed."

"For now we have to get out of here," Zyla responded.

"And go where?" Yvonna asked.

"I have a place."

CHAPTER SIXTEEN

ricks sat in the passenger seat of Amanda's car nervously. Every now and again he would look around and out each window.

"I think you can relax now," she said, shaking her head. "You been doing that for five minutes. Nobody is following us."

He looked out the back window again. "You don't know my family."

She giggled. "Oh, so I don't remember your aunt going through my purse before she let me see you the other day? Or your cousins hanging outside of your room to be sure you wouldn't leave?" She laughed again. "I know how they can be. Trust me. But I think we shook them off."

"I hope so." He wasn't buying it.

"Bricks, even if they knew you left, they have no idea where you are."

He dragged a hand down his face. "This why we always got a problem. You think you know my people but you don't. They are the streets. And when you live and breathe the streets, you know everything that goes on in them. It'll be a matter of time before they find me."

She continued to pilot the car in silence. And he was grateful because at least he could think. "Bricks, are you, I mean, do you even see me?"

His temples throbbed. "Not this again."

"If not now then—"

"I was a trash type dude back in the day. I know I was. There's no denying it. At the same time, I never lied to you. I always told you what the deal was from the gate."

"That doesn't make it hurt any less."

"And I understand all that. But I still told you the truth, and at the end of the day, that's all I owe you. That's all I owe anybody."

She nodded at first and then suddenly, whipped the car to the left and through traffic. She parked on the side of the road. "You know what, get out my car. I'm sick of you."

He frowned. "Come on, man, stop playing."

"Nah, I want you out."

"Are you fuckin' serious? You say you a grown woman and when I be straight up with you, it's a problem." He shook his head. "Drive me to the motel before I go off in this bitch."

"It ain't about you being real with me. It's about you not at least…at least…"

"What?" He yelled, interrupting her.

"At least pretend like you have a place in your heart for me." She paused. "Most women won't admit it but sometimes we prefer a lie."

"You want me to lie to you?" He laughed. "Are you that fucked up in the head? You want that much attention?"

She huffed and puffed while gripping the steering wheel tighter. Her words sounded dumb when he said them out loud. "I never got over you. Even when you were out of the country, I always remembered the time we shared." She sighed deeply. "But now I realize you never gave a fuck."

"Amanda, it's not like—."

"Get out, Bricks. I'm done with you. I'm done with all of this."

"Wow." He shook his head.

She grabbed her phone out of her purse when he wouldn't bounce. "You want me to call the police? Or Raul? Because I will if you don't leave my car."

"Okay…okay…" he thought about slapping her into the window but left instead. The moment he shut the door she pulled off, barely missing his feet.

"Fuck!" He yelled into the night.

For a moment, he thought about what would have happened if he chose to lie. But he was tired of holding secrets; he had many yet to be shared. At the same time his wife was crazy, and he knew the last thing he needed was for Yvonna to choke her to death because he was leading her on.

Nah, in his opinion it was best to tell Amanda straight up. Sure he fucked her the one time. But he was certain that if Yvonna were in the same situation, she would use the pussy as currency too.

At least he hoped so.

When Bricks made it to the motel on foot, he noticed the door had been kicked in and a worker was repairing the lock. "What happened here?" Bricks asked. He was horrified.

"What it looks like?" The elderly white man with gray hair responded.

"Listen, man, we rented this room for two weeks and I'm just trying to find out where my wife and daughter are. Now answer the fucking question."

He stood up and wiped his hands on a dingy towel hanging off his pants. "I can't say. But I'm pretty sure your wife is fine."

Bricks sighed deeply, just as Marge, Zyla's friend walked up to her room, which was directly next-door. The suspicious looks she gave Bricks put him on pause and suddenly he was interested in what she had to say.

Bricks stood outside of the motel waiting on Raul to show up. It was a big risk. He had some reservations if he should reach out; after all, he was responsible for him falling off the wagon. But he needed help and felt the chance was worth it.

Twenty minutes later, Raul pulled up in his pickup truck, shocking the hell out of Bricks who walked over to the driver's side window. "Wow…you came."

He shook his head and Bricks could smell the scent of alcohol on his breath and immediately felt remorseful. He had been drinking again. "You mean despite you fucking up my sobriety? Despite you flooding auntie's house that she loved all her life? You mean despite her crying non-stop when they told her they may have to demolish her home? Because the water damage in the walls was that bad? And she might lose everything?"

Bricks looked down as guilt made his stomach churn. He told himself he felt warranted, since they were holding him against his will and at the same time, he knew they were doing it out of love. "Yeah...I guess that's what I'm saying."

"Well I'm not like you, Bricks." He shrugged. "You my cousin. And we family. So I'm here. The rest of them would be too but you said to come alone."

Bricks felt worse. It wasn't like he didn't know his family was concrete. It just made him feel bad for making such drastic moves. "So, how I know you won't try and take me back?"

Raul laughed. "Who the fuck will have you? You done destroyed auntie's house, man. Nah, it ain't about all that. Now get the fuck in so I can take you to this crazy bitch...I mean...your wife."

CHAPTER SEVENTEEN

Yvonna was in Zyla's mother's house and ready to leave. The woman was in the earlier stages of dementia, and as a result kept coming downstairs asking who everyone was, including Zyla.

That may have been why Yvonna crept Zyla out so much. They were both out of this world in the head.

Zyla, her two brothers and a girl cousin were also in the cramped kitchen trying to get to know the crazy one called Yvonna. Marge had gone to the motel earlier to check the scene. And be sure the maintenance man on payroll quickly repaired the door and diverted police if they arrived.

Luckily outside of Bricks, no one came.

"Listen," Zyla said. "Whatever you have going on, can't be at the motel. I'm sorry that you don't get it but I'll say it again. You must bounce."

"You told me that already." Yvonna sighed. "And what kind of business you got that's so important anyway?"

"I don't have to give you details."

"Then I'm going back and let them niggas know where to find me." Yvonna rose from the kitchen chair.

"And we gonna act a fool to be sure that bitch gets closed down!"

"Okay...okay...listen..." she took a deep breath, palms in her direction.

Yvonna took a seat.

"Over the past three years, shits been bad at the motel. Corporate tired of the lawsuits and threatened to shut it down if another crime happens. If that motel closes people who know I'm there won't be able to find me."

Yvonna didn't see the controversy. "Post up in a different one and tell everybody where you are."

"I can't. I don't contact my customers on the phone and they don't contact me. Plus vendors for these delivery trucks know what I do. When they ready to make a deal, they know where to come. I gotta stay. At least for now."

"What you sell?"

"Hair." She shrugged.

Yvonna was shook. "Ain't that much weave selling in the world."

"You keep thinking that if you want. I don't give a fuck." She sighed. "Anyway I need one more year and I'll buy a legit location and legit product. Not right now."

"Well you have a problem then," Yvonna said throwing her hands up. "Because the motel is the last place my daughter saw me and I have all intentions on staying in case she comes back."

Zyla paced the floor and stopped in front of Yvonna. She couldn't stand her pretty ass. "Okay...what if we help you?"

She frowned. "You mean help me get my daughter back?"

"Nah...help you get at whoever came to the motel tonight. This not an Amber Alert operation. This is simply me assisting you so you can go back wherever the fuck you came from."

"Okay..."

Zyla looked at her brothers and cousin. They weren't too excited to get involved but they all understood Zyla's problem. Selling stolen hair netted them between fifty and twenty thousand a month. So it wasn't something they were willing to give up.

"There's one problem," Yvonna mentioned. "I don't know who's after me. It could be anybody."

Zyla removed her phone from her pocket. "Leave that to me. I know everything going in and around my motel."

"Her motel?" Gabriella said. "Now who's crazy?"

Zyla dialed a number and stepped a few feet away. "Were you able to fix the door?"

"Yeah."

"And did you find information on who kicked it down?"

"You gonna have to start giving me more money." He paused. "The little you give ain't enough to chase killers."

She was speaking with the maintenance man who ran the motel and put Zyla and her crew on to anyone causing problems around the property. If the motel owners knew how much Zyla kept crime down, in an effort to run her illegal operation, they may have put her on payroll.

"You know I got you," she said. "Now you have any information or not?"

"I have an address."

Zyla smiled. "Give me everything you know."

Yvonna sat outside on the porch using Zyla's phone. She was hoping that the man she was reaching would answer this time and luckily for her he did. "Jabar, it's me again."

He laughed. She was relentless. But that's what he loved about her. "What you want?"

The moment Yvonna heard his voice she knew he was no longer angry as he was when she first reached out. She was successful at wearing a nigga down. "I know you don't wanna talk still."

"You got five minutes."

"Okay...okay...I'm...I'm in trouble."

"What's new?" He chuckled once. "It's also the only time you call."

"I know you hate me, but I separated from you, or left you back in the day, because I didn't want this lifestyle for you. I didn't want you to go through what I'm going through now. But I always cared."

Silence.

She needed to reach deeper.

"Jabar, you right about me. I can be selfish. But my daughter...she...she doesn't deserve what's happening. I mean can you at least help me get her back? If you ever cared at all?"

Silence.

"Jabar...you there?"

"Give me the address."

With help on the way, Yvonna felt an immediate sense of relief. Because even with Zyla's crew providing lookout once they made it to Cinnamon's, it was clear they weren't going to kill anybody if shit got heated. And she believed them. She needed manpower on her side.

She needed Jabar.

"You know this a mistake right?" Gabriella said, appearing to her right. "You feel it and yet you still don't want to hear what I have to say."

"I don't need your help. In case you haven't realized it already, I have people looking out for me now."

"You aren't thinking straight. This won't go as you plan."

Yvonna ignored her and walked back into the house. Zyla was standing before her and she got worried. "What?"

"Who were you talking to?"

"What you want?"

Zyla rolled her eyes. The crazy chick was cringy as fuck. "Your husband here. I remember him from the motel."

"What? How he know where I was?"

"Marge. Now you coming or not?"

A minute later Yvonna walked out and up to Bricks who sat in the truck with Raul. His eyes said he still hated her.

"Bae, what you doing here?"

Bricks hopped out and hugged Yvonna tightly. "Hey, Squeeze!"

"What *you* doing here?" She asked again, kissing him all over his face. "I...I don't understand. I thought your family didn't want you helping me."

"I know but—."

Suddenly Jabar pulled up in a silver Benz blasting music. Yvonna's stomach immediately dropped. Feeling lightheaded, she hoped this would end well. Bricks was the murdering type and so was Jabar.

So she couldn't be sure.

Is this what Gabriella meant when she alluded that trouble was near?

Bricks caught her mood change. "You know that nigga?"

"Just...just stay right here. Please." She walked toward Jabar's car.

"See, she still up to her same shit," Raul said to Bricks, taking a sip of Wild Irish Rose.

Bricks rolled his eyes.

Yvonna slid into Jabar's car. "Who that?" Jabar asked looking out the back window. Bricks was staring at his vehicle hard. "Your husband?"

"I'm gonna get rid of him."

"That's not what I asked." He glared. "Is it your husband or not?"

"Yes."

He shook his head and sighed. "Can't say I don't deserve this shit. I should've left you alone like I did when you pulled up to my house."

She placed her hand over his and he was done.

He loved her too much to fight anymore.

"I need your help. And if we stick together, this will be over sooner than later." She paused. "Please, Jabar, don't leave me now."

"Aight, but when this is done, I'm gonna be pushing for you to choose me. I hope you understand that."

CHAPTER EIGHTEEN
FRIDAY

Cinnamon was angry that the call to the motel ended in vain. He had a feeling he was in the right place, even though the room was empty. But could he be wrong?

Since he didn't have Yvonna in his trunk, it appeared he was.

Still, he had one more golden egg downstairs and it was Delilah.

He was sitting on the sofa with his wife between his legs as he pressed a lace front wig along her scalp line. It was layered with glue. Although all alpha, when it came to her chocolaty pretty ass there really wasn't much he wouldn't do.

Including help her melt her wig.

Not all of the men in her family thought she was so cute at the time.

Her nephews were in the kitchen mixing potato salad for the family reunion tomorrow and they had an attitude about it. "Aunt Ginger, how much longer you gonna be doing your hair?" The Youngest Nephew asked. "You been forever."

By Reign

"I'm coming!" She said. "And stop being lazy. It ain't like I didn't put everything in the bowl. All ya'll gotta do is mix it." She shook her head.

"Keep still," Cinnamon said applying the lace with precision. "I don't want you mad at me if this don't...what you call it again?"

"Melt." She giggled and settled down.

Everyone was on edge.

They had a house full of people coming tomorrow for the family reunion and she could tell he wasn't in the mood. Especially after going to the motel only for Yvonna to be nowhere in sight. Not only that, but the squad had given up trust in him and decided to leave the matter alone.

For now anyway.

"How you doing?" She asked.

He shrugged. "I'm mad but what can I do? She got away. Again." He continued stating the obvious.

"So you really gonna keep the girl here? You know nothing will stop my aunts from going downstairs. Even if you tell them it's off limits."

He knew she was right.

He had told them several times in the past that the basement was his private space. His man cave. But when they popped up on uninvited visits, they would always hush him and find excuses to invade his area. Just to be nosey. Believing he was a drug dealer.

Whether taking a personal call, or checking for mildew, it was always a reason.

"She won't be here." He said.

"Why?"

"I'm gonna kill her." He admitted.

She looked up at him. "What?"

"You heard me."

"But that wasn't the plan, Cinnamon." She stood up and continued to press her lace front so that it would stay in place.

"I hear you."

"It ain't about hearing me. I don't agree with this shit. If you kill her daughter, she will hunt us for life. We will never be at peace. "

"I have to, Ginger." He leaned back. "You said it yourself. Your people will find a reason to go downstairs and there ain't no explaining why we got a girl tied up with a sack to the face. Don't worry. I'll make it quick and painless."

"So we'll cancel the reunion," she said excitedly. "That way you won't have to do it."

He chuckled. "Even if you tried to cancel you know they'd still show up. Talking about they *done made all*

this food and shit. Trust me, there is no other way. She must go."

The idea of someone dying outside of Yvonna Harris had never entered her mind, and still it made sense. He had obsessed over Yvonna most of his life. Since she'd known him. And she hoped now, if the girl was dead, he'd get over it so they could move on with their lives.

She sat on his lap, straddle style and placed a cool hand on his face. "Cinnamon, can you at least do it outside the house? That way — "

"Don't ask me something you know I can't do." He looked deeply into her eyes. "Somebody might see me. You know your husband, I will be safe."

"I do but — ."

CRASH!

When they heard a loud noise out in front of their house, he erratically shoved her off his lap as they both hustled to the living room window. At the same time, her three nephews came running behind them, all trying to see what caused the commotion.

A young woman was out front, with her hands on both sides of her face, the front end of her car crashed into the back of his truck. She appeared in shock. "Sorry...sorry...sorry."

"What the fuck?" He yelled running outside, his entourage closely behind. "Fuck you do to my shit?" He roared running up to her, hands in tight knots.

His wife's nephews circled the truck assessing the damage. "This looks bad, unc," Nephew One said. "You ain't gonna be able to buff this out." He laughed, thinking it was a joke.

"I'm so sorry," the woman with the bohemian locs said. "I...I didn't see your truck."

"Fuck you mean you ain't see my truck?" He continued. "It ain't invisible. It's right fucking here!" He shoved his nephews away and walked around his SUV, stepping on glass shards from his broken windows.

As they continued to talk about the damage, his wife had an eerie feeling in the pit of her gut. Something felt off. "Cinnamon," she said in a low voice.

He didn't hear her. As most men who have experienced damage to their prize rides, his mind was on the condition of his vehicle and how much it would cost to be repaired.

"Cinnamon!" She yelled louder, looking up and down the dark street. "This doesn't feel right."

As if the light was finally clicked on in his mind, he turned to his family and yelled, "Get in the house!"

Zyla smiled, jumped in her car and sped off into the night. Besides, her work was done.

Now in the confines of his house, he realized his error by stepping out of his home without thinking straight. The nephews and his wife sat on the sofa, as he paced the floor in front of them.

"Did you see anything weird?" He locked the front door and stood in front of her again. "To make you think something was up?"

"No...it just seems odd. Almost like she hit the truck on purpose to get us to come out."

He was angry but his mind told him she was right. If someone wanted to draw him outside, hitting his ride would be the best way. But where was the ambush? Was it possible that his wife saved them before things got out of control?

Cinnamon walked toward his cell phone in the kitchen. "I'ma call my dudes and —."

"Sit down, my man," Bricks said, walking into the living room, gun aimed at him.

He felt gut punched.

Ginger was right.

He let his guards down.

Feeling safe in his own home, because in his mind Yvonna had no idea which of the many enemies was coming for her, he had left his gun in his bedroom and his cell in the kitchen.

Bricks walked over to the front door and unlocked it as Jabar walked inside. He was also aiming a gun in their direction. Yvonna tried her best to get rid of Bricks earlier that day but he made his point clear. After being separated from her, there was no way he was leaving her side again, especially not with another nigga willing and able in the midst.

"What ya'll want?" Cinnamon yelled, trying to put on as if he was in control.

"Nah, the question is what do you want?" Yvonna said, switching out of the kitchen. Her eyes were shielded with shades and her spiked hair was teased to perfection. The sexier she was, the more dangerous she was for all involved.

When Zyla slammed the car into Cinnamon's truck, she was confident enough to know that the distraction would be large enough that everyone would exit the house.

She was right.

With everybody outside, Yvonna and Bricks could ease inside. With Zyla's crew's assistance.

He shook his head. "Wow...I can't believe this shit." He took a deep breath. "You got the nerve to be coming over my house? When you know how badly I want you?"

"Well consider my presence a gift." She said. "Now where is my daughter?"

"I don't know what you talking about." He folded his arms over his chest arrogantly.

BOOM.

Bricks shot one of the nephews, leaving two alive.

Cinnamon felt dizzy with rage and he finally understood why most feared her. When she was in the revenge state, she wasn't about playing games. "Where is my daughter?" She repeated.

"Listen, I really don't —."

BOOM!

Bricks shot another nephew and his wife passed out, rolling on the floor.

Yvonna stepped closer. "Where is my daughter?"

"If you kill my family I won't —."

BOOM.

All of the rage and arrogance Cinnamon held diminished as he began to tremble. His family was growing smaller by the bullet. Dead nephews at his feet. "Where is she?"

Bricks aimed at his unconscious wife.

"Downstairs! She's downstairs!"

With both guns trained on him, she tiptoed down the dark stairway leading into the basement. She could hear her heart beat thump in her ears. Just seeing her daughter would make everything she'd gone through over the week better. But first she had to make sure she was okay.

If a hair on her head was harmed, she would tear his face to the bone.

Walking up to a chair, she saw a figure seated with a potato sack over its head. When she lifted the mask, her heart dropped when she saw the face of a person she didn't know. Taking the gag out of the girl's mouth she angrily asked, "Who the fuck are you?"

The young girl smiled. "You must be Yvonna. They told me so much about you."

Yvonna glared harder. "Don't play with me, who the fuck are you?"

"I'm Lisa." She smiled. "My mother's name is Courtney."

Yvonna looked at the red halter-top she was wearing and frowned. Now that she thought about it, she remembered her from the doctor's office. She

hadn't seen the blouse when she first descended the steps because she was focused on her face.

It was baby whore.

"Did you tell them you were my daughter?"

She smiled.

"Why you do that?"

"My daddy is mean to me. He only wants to spend time with his girlfriend. I figured if I was missing he would be scared and — ."

"They could have killed you! Are you that stupid that you don't understand?"

She trembled. "But…if he did, my daddy would be sad." She was way out of touch with reality. Which was why she was seeing a psychiatrist. "Then he would miss me more."

"They think you left with your friends. On a drunk binge. Nobody cares."

Tears rolled down the girl's face. "Can you take me home? My daddy might be plenty worried now."

Yvonna hated her and contemplated taking her life for the games.

"Can you take me home?" She continued to beg and it was at that time that she resembled a child. "I'm ready to go now."

Yvonna started to say fuck her, but she remembered the Nice Receptionist and her promise to pay it forward.

So she would do just that.

But it would be the last time she would offer charity for the night.

Yvonna walked back up the stairs with Lisa, mentally wrecked. She placed the sack over the girl's face, so she couldn't see the bodies on the floor.

"Who that?" Bricks asked, confused. He was sure they would be on their way back to the Philippines before the end of the night.

Cinnamon frowned. "It's your daughter!" He said hoping things wouldn't escalate. "She told me so herself. Take the sack off and look at her face!"

She was not Delilah and Yvonna looked at Jabar. "Can you take her outside?"

He nodded and led the blindfolded girl out the door.

One gun was enough.

Yvonna shook her head, "This was all for nothing." She told Cinnamon. "You should've let shit go."

"You should've let shit go! You took a real nigga off the streets. Somebody who was like a father to us. And you thought that shit was gonna ride? You thought you would be able to get away with it? Huh?"

"That same man that you worshipped killed many himself. He wasn't no saint. He was just another nigga, like you."

She looked at Bricks. She was done talking. At the end of the day she owed him zero explanation. And every word wasted precious time. "Kill 'em. And his wife too. Don't need nobody else looking for me."

Yvonna walked outside, with the sound of two gunshots ringing behind her.

CHAPTER NINETEEN

Yvonna was sitting on the edge of the bed in her motel room talking to Jabar on the phone. Bricks had gone to get them something to eat although she wasn't in the mood for food. But after explaining that she hadn't eaten in two days, he wouldn't hear of it any other way.

Jabar had taken Courtney within five blocks of her house and dropped her off on the street. Yvonna's reason for giving the order to get her off Cinnamon's property was simple. She didn't want her around where Bricks laid out five bodies.

But to say she hated the girl was an understatement.

"I just put her out."

"Thank you again, Jabar," she sighed. "I know you didn't sign up for this but...I just...thank you. That's all I want to say."

He breathed deeply. "Will I see you again?"

"I don't know. Can that be okay for now?"

He laughed. "I don't got a choice do I? I can't get you out my system. And God knows I tried."

"I just don't wanna lie to you no more. If we do anything, I don't want lying to be our story."

"I get it. And I got respect for it too." He paused. "But can I tell you something?"

"Yes, of course."

"I don't trust your husband."

She frowned and moved uneasily on the bed. It squeaked. "Why?"

"I don't know…just don't."

She sighed deeply. He had ulterior motives and so she couldn't take his phrase at face value. "I gotta go, Jabar. Thanks again. I'll call before I head back overseas."

"I'm gonna hold you to it. I need to hear your voice one more time."

When she hung up she tossed herself back on the bed and Gabriella crawled on top of her. At the moment the bullet wound stung. Bricks had asked her repeatedly who shot her but she refused to tell. Make no mistake, when she got Delilah, she had plans for the shooters herself.

"What do you want?" Yvonna asked, looking up at her.

"Are you ready to hear what I have to say?"

Yvonna's temples throbbed. Her chore to find Delilah ended in vain. And so Gabriella had her right where she wanted. She had to listen, which essentially meant she had to listen to herself.

"Go ahead."

"Look at her computer."

Yvonna frowned. "What you mean?"

"Open Delilah's laptop and go through it." She paused. "Trust me, you'll find out everything you want to know."

"I'm not invading her privacy. Besides, she's the victim."

"No such thing as a victim since we all sin." Gabriella got up and stood next to the drawer. "All the answers are there. You know they are, because I am you and if I'm saying it, it's on your mind."

Yvonna sat up and looked at the dresser. Standing up, she opened the drawer and put the laptop on the bed. Curious, she pulled out the pink glitter MacBook and opened it wide.

The screen glowed against her skin. It was password protected and she tried several codes, all were incorrect. "Fuck," she said to herself.

"Think," Gabriella said, whispering into her ear. "You know your daughter. You know the password. So think out the box."

Yvonna entered a few more and again she received an incorrect password error. She had one more chance or she would risk locking the computer. She didn't know what inspired her next code, but for some reason she entered the name:

BILAL

She gained immediate access.

Her heart sank.

Bilal, was the name of Yvonna's first true love. He was the man who sent her on a revenge spree. He was also the person who slept with her best friend Sabrina; resulting in a son she would give the same name. Yvonna had never told Delilah about him, or her past, so how did she know his name?

For a second her mind went back to the time she last saw Bilal Jr.

YEARS AGO

Yvonna was nervous as she waited for Bilal, Jr. to appear on the other side of the glass. He was in jail and she was in disguise while visiting.

She was wearing a long brown wig, large black-rimmed glasses and zero makeup so that those who wanted her dead would not see her face. She always kept a fake ID on her so it was easy to see him without being detected, not to mention he hadn't been transferred to prison yet for his recent crimes. The jail had more leniencies.

She had to see him but at the same time she couldn't believe how skittish she was, he was just a child. At the same time, in an effort to go on with her life, she had to kill more people and most of them were in and around his life. She had already destroyed his world by killing his mother, father and grandmother.

Thanks to her, he had no one.

But this wasn't her plan.

The moment she saw his face, she couldn't get over how much he looked just like his father. As a matter of fact, since

he was older, he looked exactly like Bilal the last time she saw him.

When Bilal Jr. picked up the phone, she followed suit.

"Thanks for retaining my lawyer." He looked at the table under him, instead of into her eyes. "But I'm confused on why you did it." He faced her. "One minute you trying to kill me and the next you want to help me out. Why?"

"I know it's confusing, Bilal. I don't understand a lot of this either. Just know that you and I are connected in more ways than you realize. And it was my responsibility to help you get out of here. And to right a few wrongs. In all of my life, you're the only one I truly regret hurting."

He frowned. "Why you say that?"

"When I was younger, I murdered your father. I didn't know until years later, that it was triggered after I overheard him talking to your mother on the phone. She wanted him to leave me. He just proposed to me and I must've been consumed with jealousy. So I took his life, and I'm so sorry, Bilal. I truly am. When it happened I thought it was my father who committed the crime, but it was actually me. I'm sick, sicker than a lot of people realize, and I'm just understanding why."

"I'm confused."

"I suffer from multiple personality disorder. It's plagued me all of my life." She swallowed. "And the night of your father's death, I was so dead set on revenge that I didn't think about how life would end up for you." Tears rolled down her face. "It wasn't enough for me to murder him. Mad at the world, I murdered your mother and your grandmother too." She looked into his eyes. "And for the first time in my life, I want to say I'm sorry. The way your life ended up is my biggest regret."

Bilal, Jr.'s cheeks trembled and his eyes were red and teary. "You left me with nobody." He balled his fists up and stared at them. "You left me with nothing."

"I know. And I'm sorry." She looked at him intently. "I did to you, what they did to me." Her watch beeped indicating she had thirty minutes to make it to the strip to fly out of the country, or risk getting left. "Look, I know you can never see it in your heart to forgive me, but I hope you'll try to accept my apology. I just wanted you to know that none of the things that happened to you was your fault, including being in here. It's all mine."

"Did you kill my twin brothers too?"

She wasn't directly responsible. But Bricks and Swoopes told her about the situation, but she didn't want him to know they were involved. Because it would look as if she were involved too. "No." She lied. "I didn't have nothing to do with that."

"I've been waiting to talk to you alone. I wondered what I'd say to you and how I would feel. And now that the time has come, I don't have the emotions I thought I would." He focused on the ceiling. "I don't know what to say to you, Yvonna. I'm confused..."

"Say whatever you feel."

He sighed. "Okay," he tapped his knuckles on the desk. "I would like to say thank you for paying for my attorney, because when I get out of here, I'm going to spend the rest of my life looking for you." He pressed his finger against the glass, leaving his sweaty print behind. "You haven't seen the last of me, bitch so I hope you're a good hider. Now get the fuck out of my face." He got up, dropped the phone and left her alone.

After Yvonna remembered how she ruined the boy's life, and the last words he said to her, she wondered if it was possible that Bilal Jr. got a hold of Delilah, and then she found all the correspondences between the screen name *LonelyInTheP* and the screen name JustLikeMyP in her computer.

She reasoned 'Lonely In P' actually meant, *lonely in the Philippines* and 'Just Like My P' stood for, *Just like my pops*. So she scanned through the messages and within seconds, all of her questions were answered.

In a gist, Bilal, fresh out of prison, due to the lawyer Yvonna secured for him, spent months looking for Delilah and Yvonna. He had scanned Filipino sites at first but then went to more popular social media sites, looking for foreigners who were in the country alone.

It took two years, but with some time and much effort, he found her and together they plotted to do *something* that would warrant Delilah coming back to the states. That *something* involved her falling out the window, and onto bushes, coupled with depression.

Everything was planned.

And it worked.

Once back in the states, he took her out of the doctor's office willingly.

It was true. Silva did see Yvonna and her daughter before he went to Cinnamon. But in his anxiousness, he didn't see Delilah's face. What he did see was the jean jacket she was wearing.

So when he went back to the doctor's office, after telling Cinnamon, he grabbed the girl he saw. Lisa, who was wearing a halter top and a jean jacket around her waist.

Pulling up to her in his Escalade while Lisa was texting outside, Silva said, "What's your name?"

He was attractive and she had daddy issues, so she humored the much older man in the expensive car. "My name is whatever you want it to be."

He didn't have time for games. "Are you Delilah or not?"

She leaned on his car window. "Y...yeah, why so serious?"

He unlocked his door. "Good, come with me."

This one act of mistaken identity, threw Yvonna off the right track for days. She never, ever, saw Delilah being a part of the dilemma and yet it all made sense.

Yvonna was still scanning the messages when she came to another journal entry. What she saw brought her to tears. It was the single event that led Delilah to wanting to leave the country, which pushed her right into the arms of Bilal Jr.

And it broke her heart in ways she didn't know were possible.

CHAPTER TWENTY

ilal Jr. tried to calm down his uncles and aunts but it was getting hard. At the end of the day the only thing they wanted was to kill the young girl that Bilal, although much older, and in his twenties, now deemed *his girl.*

But their hate for Yvonna ran deep.

After all, Yvonna had killed their sibling, Treyana, along with her twin nephews who were also Bilal's brothers, Lazer and Uzi. And now the remaining siblings wanted revenge.

Treyana's siblings were Gabe, Hall, Easter, Tabitha, Tahir and Oakes. In their day and even with age, they were the epitome of everything wrong with the hood. In fact, they were so ratchet that if you put the first letters in their name together they would spell GHETTO. And before Treyana died she was no better.

Ironically, after Lazer and Uzi were killed, due to Yvonna and her crew, the family ousted Bilal just because. But it was Easter's death, due to a beating she succumbed to by the hands of Bilal, which they didn't know about, that brought him back in connection with his aunts and uncles. They believed it was best to stick together to avenge their family members deaths. After all, there was power in numbers.

And they needed his pretty face.

So naturally when he made them aware that he successfully lured fourteen-year-old Delilah out of the Philippines and to the states, they awarded him for his efforts by allowing him back into the fold.

But now he was putting on as if he cared about her, which was not part of the plan.

Bilal Jr. was in his bedroom talking to Delilah who was happy just being around him. Her only problem was that since they'd been together, he seemed distant and she couldn't understand why.

He was playing a video game in his room, while looking at the door constantly when she jumped on his lap. "So, when we going to fuck? Because I been thinking about you since—."

She was a whole virgin so he shoved her off. "Why you talking like that? I don't like it."

She frowned. "What is up with you? Every time I try to touch you, you reject me."

"I'm not rejecting you...I'm...you just don't understand."

"Why you different, B?"

"What you talking about?"

"When we first met you kept swearing by all the stuff you would do to me when we hooked up. Now that I'm here you don't treat me the same." She pouted. "I could've stayed in the Philippines if I knew it would be all this."

"I'm sick of you throwing that shit up in my face."

"Then talk to me." She cried. "Please."

"You acting like a kid."

Hearing her age thrown in her face enraged her. She was concerned that him being in his early twenties and her being fourteen would be a problem. And now she was finding out it was true.

"Bilal, I'm not a kid."

"You are a kid. So chill out before —."

The bedroom door opened and Gabe stepped inside. "Let me talk to you for a minute."

"Hi, Gabe," Delilah waved, hoping to gain his respect.

He nodded at her as they walked out and into the kitchen, where Hall, Tabitha, Tahir and Oakes were waiting.

Not every man in the room was a Bilal fan.

Tabitha didn't say anything at first but she was grilling Bilal with her eyes. Despite reconciliation, she hated him. In her mind, the only reason they were connected was because Bilal senior was his father and the father of the twins. She personally saw no reason to keep him around now that they had Delilah.

"What's up?" Bilal asked.

"I think we may have to move her." Gabe said.

"Move her where? And why?" He scratched his beautiful black curly hair.

"See that's your problem," Tabitha said pointing a narrow finger his way. "You don't listen."

"I do but—."

"If you listened then you'd remember me telling you that Cinnamon and his crew were looking for Delilah too."

Bilal shrugged. "You told me but why should we care now?"

"You should care about everything we tell you." Gabe said. "Shit about to get serious."

He wasn't making sense. "This is starting to get on my nerves." Bilal said.

"How 'bout you be quiet, lil nigga." Tabitha snapped. "Show some fucking respect."

Bilal glared. She looked for the worthless of things to fight about. He wasn't the same seventeen-year-old kid he was when they first met. He was a man who didn't feel the need to be disrespected anymore.

"You got something you wanna say to me, Tabitha?" He asked, stepping up to her. "'Cause if you do, just say it."

The rest of the siblings jumped between them, stopping whatever was about to pop off.

The way Bilal saw it was simple. He had already killed their sister Easter by beating her with his bare hands, forcing her in a coma that would eventually take her life. He had no problems doing it again. Had they known he was responsible, instead of the robbers he told them about, he wouldn't even exist.

"Everybody calm down," Gabe said. He focused back on Bilal. "We should care because Cinnamon and 'em thought they had Delilah. Tabitha been keeping in contact with some niggas who know them. Well he dead now."

Bilal frowned. "How?"

"You know how. She must've got a hold of him. It's just a matter of time before she starts looking for her daughter again. At this house. I figure we got a few days but I want to move early."

"Let me ask you something, when we kill Yvonna, you leaving Delilah out of it right?"

"Nah." Tabitha smiled. "She'll be the second to go."

This caused Bilal's heart to rock although he didn't understand why. In the beginning he knew he wanted to get at Yvonna. And he knew he needed Delilah to do it. But something about Delilah had him feeling some kind of way.

In a sense, he was falling in love with the kiddo.

"I don't think we got to kill her."

"We do." Gabe said. "When its time, you can go through with it right? Because we all the family you got."

CHAPTER TWENTY-ONE

When Bricks came back with the Chinese food, he froze when he saw the look on Yvonna's face. He knew it was time to come clean. "Why?" She asked, as tears rolled down her cheek. Her voice was barely above a whisper but he heard her loud and clear.

He placed the food on the table and walked across from her. Leaning against the wall. "Baby, I—."

"Tell me the fucking truth!" She trembled punching a fist into her palm. "No more...no more lies."

He took a deep breath and sat on the edge of the bed. "Living in the Philippines, it's been, it's been hard on me. And I...I didn't know how to come to you because, your mind and the way...the way it works."

She frowned. "Fuck is that supposed to mean?"

"You haven't been well."

"What you talking about? I, I been taking medicine. My mind is—."

"The neighbors you see aren't real...the visitors we invite over for dinner aren't real...I allowed you to figure shit out but for the most part, you been worse.

And the kids know it, they're just too embarrassed to say anything."

Her eyes widened. Ming was right. "No...that's not true."

"I won't lie about some shit like this, I swear to God."

"But, I haven't seen Gabriella before today. She's—."

His body tensed.

He knew the name.

Well.

Fear hit him. "Wait...she's back?"

She felt stupid, ridiculous and hurt. If what he was saying was true, she had been living in a state of lies with him as her enabler. Why didn't he tell her she was insane?

"I know what you're doing." She sniffled, and wiped her nose with the back of her hand. "You...you want me to believe this is all my fault."

"That's the last thing I want, Yvonna. I take full responsibility for what I've done. But, I have to tell you how, how confused shit got that night. Because you have to believe me when I say, if I wasn't in my right mind, what happened, could never have gone down."

"You mean the fact that you're a fucking alcoholic? And the fact that I had to drag your ass in most nights because you couldn't even walk? All because you miss home?"

"Yes."

"So what part of this has to do with you fucking my daughter?!"

Eww. Hearing that hit hard.

"What part, Bricks?"

He knew the day would come where he had to tell her what happened, but he didn't think he would feel so weak. "You were out, at the church down the street. Trying to pray the slayings away."

"Bricks!"

"I had been drinking and...and wanting to go home. She came in, wearing your red silk robe with the black bat on the back that you love so much. The one that keeps you cool when —"

"I know the fucking robe!"

He looked down. "She walked in and all I saw...all I saw was the robe. I didn't...I couldn't see anything else, Yvonna. I swear to God. You have to believe me."

"What happened?" She asked through clenched teeth.

"She...she kissed me."

Yvonna's body heaved as she cried harder. "I...I can't believe this...I...I can't believe this is happening."

"She got on top of me and...and the moment my hands touched her waist, the moment I felt her, I knew she wasn't you. And I pushed her away. But she wouldn't stop pursuing me. She wouldn't stop trying to get at me and I wanted to be gone. I wanted to come back here."

"You have broken my heart more than you can ever imagine."

"I wanted to tell you. I tried and you would stop me each time. I even tried on the plane on the way over but you wouldn't listen. I don't know if you thought I was going to bring up going home and tried to avoid me. I don't know baby, but I wanted to talk to you." He got up and stood on his knees between her legs. "I'm so fucking sorry. I'm so...so sorry."

"You knew my secrets." She shook her head slowly as she looked down at him. "You knew what I been through and you do the same to my daughter?" She smashed the side of his face with a palm.

"No!" He yelled standing up. "I didn't. I didn't...didn't...molest her repeatedly. I didn't...I didn't take her body like them niggas at AFCOG did you. She was young and she made a mistake and I corrected that shit. Quick!"

"You entered her body, Bricks," she said softly. "Tell the truth. That's what you mean when you say the moment you *felt* her you knew she wasn't me. Isn't it true?"

"I pushed her away. She's a child, who made a mistake. What more could I do?"

He was right but it still hurt. "She sees the act as rejection," she responded with her head low. "And what you did that night led her to Bilal, someone who wants to kill me because I took away everyone he loves." She wiped the tears away.

"I'm sorry." He was being genuine but it couldn't be received.

"Why do all the men I love have fault? Do I really gravitate toward what hates me the most?"

"Yvonna, I—."

She picked up the phone and dialed a number. "Come in."

A minute later a knock rapped on the door and she opened it as Jabar walked inside. He was armed and aimed in Bricks' direction.

It really was his pleasure.

"Keep an eye on him. Zyla and the others are next door if you need 'em."

He nodded and handed her the keys to his car. "I left something for you, already packed and loaded, in the glove compartment."

Yvonna took a deep breath, walked toward the door and grabbed the cool knob. Looking down she said, "I wanted so much to be happy. I wanted, I wanted so much to see what it meant to be, to be domesticated." She looked back at Bricks. "But I ain't no real housewife. And I'm not here to experience heaven on earth. Now I know that I am all the bad parts. And I'm okay with it."

"Baby, please don't—."

She walked out, leaving him alone with Jabar.

CHAPTER TWENTY-TWO

In bed, Delilah was deep in sleep when she was nudged by Bilal. "Get up, bae." He whispered in her ear. "And don't make a sound. We have to get out of here."

She wiped hair out of her face. "What...what's going on?" She yawned.

"I can't tell you right now."

Crawling on her knees, she sat on the edge of the bed. "Well at least turn the lights on so I can see my stuff."

He grabbed her by the arms and stared down at her. He was serious and wanted her to feel him. "Get ya shit and let's get the fuck out of here. I'm not fucking around."

Hearing the urgency in his voice, finally she understood that whatever had him shook was not a laughing matter. So she got up as quickly as she could and grabbed her clothing that was scattered about the floor. When she was dressed, she grabbed his hand.

Eager to leave, he squeezed her fingertips so tightly, they began to numb. When he was ready, he pulled the door open and a slice of light shined through the doorway. He peeked out and when he believed the coast was clear, he crept toward the front door.

"Where you going?" Tabitha asked, smiling behind them. She had stepped out from one of the bedrooms.

Bilal snatched Delilah as they moved hurriedly toward the front door but when they opened it, Gabe and the others were standing outside on the step smoking.

"Get back inside." Gabe said pointing at the house. He flicked his cigarette. "You not going anywhere, young bull."

"Please, man, don't do this."

"If you wanna leave, bounce, but you not taking our bait with you."

"Bilal, can you, can you tell me what's going on?" Delilah asked. "Because I'm scared."

Sitting in the living room, Delilah was weighed heavy in the mind.

After all, she had just learned that her mother had been responsible for over one hundred deaths and yet she didn't understand how it was possible. Yvonna had preached so much about love and respecting herself that Delilah believed she was a saint.

Now she was learning that she was all that was wrong with the world. Of course she remembered Yvonna talking to herself at the house. But she talked to herself too.

And this trait was something she didn't share with Bilal because it was too scary for words.

"I don't believe you," Delilah said to Gabe as a single tear trailed down her cheek. "I don't believe...I don't believe any of you."

"It doesn't matter." Tabitha said.

"Sure doesn't." Tahir said. "At the end of the day we ain't got no reason to lie. Your mother is a devil and she will go down."

"Bilal," she said, voice trembling. "Are they...are they lying?"

"Tell her the other part too," Gabe interrupted. "Tell her what she did to you and your people."

Bilal adjusted his stance. "She killed, she killed my mother, father, and grandmother. Then she had some niggas kill my brothers."

Her mouth opened but no words could form. "So you, you never loved me?"

"What you think, idiot?" Tabitha laughed. "I gotta say, for you to be Yvonna's daughter you aren't really that bright."

"Ain't no reason to be mean," Bilal said.

"It ain't about being mean." Tabitha continued. "What she thought, she was living in the Philippines in paradise for no reason?" She giggled. "Oh wait, you do realize you're American right? Or do you think you're Filipino too?"

Bilal stomped up to her. "Cut it out, bitch." He yelled pointing in her face.

"You need to relax." Gabe said.

"Okay…just…just let me talk to her."

"Sorry, nephew," Gabe responded. "But I can't do that."

"I'm not your nephew remember?" He snapped. "And I'm not going nowhere. You can stay outside if you want…I just, I just wanna talk to her alone."

Gabe looked at Bilal. "You got five minutes."

"Wait, you're seriously gonna let them be alone?" Tabitha asked.

"Get up and come on." Gabe said to Tabitha. "It ain't like they 'bout to fuck. I can look at them eyes and tell she's still a virgin."

"But—."

"Get the fuck up!" Gabe yelled at her. Everyone rose. And just like that the room was empty.

Now alone, Bilal sat next to Delilah and grabbed her hand. "You okay?"

She was trembling. "Bilal, why didn't you, why didn't you tell me this?"

"Because I needed you here."

"Why? So you can hurt me?"

"No, of course not."

"Then why?"

"Ever since I lost my family I felt like, like I had to get back at somebody. And the only person I could think of that deserved all my rage was your mother."

"Bilal," she touched his hand. "Please don't do this." She looked behind him in the direction where Gabe and the others went. And although she couldn't see their faces, she saw their shadows and knew they were listening through open doorways. She scooted closer. "If we stay I will die. So let's get out of here, please. While we still can."

CHAPTER TWENTY-THREE

In the motel, Bricks sat on the bed, across from Jabar who was still aiming a gun in his direction. He didn't like anything about him from the moment he pulled up in a Benz at Zyla's mother's house. "You ever seen an ice cream truck? Pink with black butterflies?"

"Yeah."

Bricks didn't know what he expected but it certainly wasn't yes. To be honest, he was just making small talk in an attempt to feel him out. Now that he had information on the truck he had plans to hunt, he readjusted a little. "Who owns it?"

Jabar smiled. "Don't worry about it."

Bricks glared. Even if it wasn't today, he had a goal to press the nigga in the ground until he told him what he wanted to know. "You think you smart, but I'm onto you."

Jabar chuckled once. "Oh yeah?"

"This all apart of your little plan ain't it?"

"You don't know shit 'bout me."

"I know you not in the habit of holding guns on niggas without reason. Unless something is in it for you. So tell me, what you really want?"

"Don't be mad at me," he said. "I'm not the one who tried to fuck my wife's daughter. I—."

"You in love with my wife ain't you?"

Jabar shifted a little in his chair and raised his aim. "She's an old friend." He cleared his throat.

"So that's what they call it now? A friend."

"Yeah."

Bricks shook his head. "You know, there's something about the crazy ones that just...that just...makes your dick hard." He laughed remembering how Yvonna roped him years ago. "It's like you can't get enough of them. Like fresh cookies straight out the oven."

"You talk wild but you have no idea who I am," he said softly.

"Fuck that supposed to mean?"

"I've always been there," he said quietly. "Before you. And I was there, outside her building, the evening she killed Bilal." He chuckled once to himself as he remembered the night. "She was wearing these red high heel shoes, chewing gum and carrying grocery bags to her apartment building."

"And..." Bricks shrugged.

"She was only nineteen back then," he continued, ignoring him. "I said, *'You need help, shawty?'* And she said, '*Naw I'm good.*'" He laughed harder, as if he could see the night on a movie screen. "She told me not to waste my time and I called her a *half crazy ass*. She hated that shit."

"Who wouldn't?"

"I knew it and I didn't care. But now that I think about it, I know calling her names was my way to get her to look at me. Because if she looked at me, if she saw me, at least she would know I was still there."

"So you think just 'cause you were around back then it means something to Yvonna?"

"My nigga, it means everything to Yvonna. That's why I'm here. Because as she went through the years, getting revenge, hunting niggas down, she always came back to me. The same nigga she told, '*Boy, don't waste your time dreamin' 'bout it. Cuz it's never gonna happen.*' The thing is, it did happen. Over and over. And I knew all I had to do was wait and that eventually the rest of you niggas would phase out."

"You can't have my wife."

"You need to be worrying about breathing right now." Jabar nodded. "I could have an accident and pull this trigger."

"I got a million lives," Bricks grinned. "Trust me, I'm not even worried."

Yvonna pulled up slowly.

She remembered the address and as she glanced down at the list in her lap she shook her head. On it were the names of Treyana's siblings, who she now realized she should have killed many years ago. Having a daughter, and something to lose softened her heart and she hated that about herself.

The names were:

Gabe

Hall

Tabitha

Tahir

Oakes

She always believed in her heart that her killers, at least one of them, would come from Treyana's family. Bilal was connected to them. After all, she had done enough damage to last the rest of their lives. But what she was not going to do was allow them to harm her daughter.

By Reign

Parking her car, she looked at the house and took a deep breath. The home was dark and the lights were out but she knew someone was inside.

They were always inside.

She looked at herself in the rearview mirror.

Gabriella was in the backseat smiling. "Awwwn," she said as if she were sad. "I'm so sorry you have to go through this."

"You're not sorry."

Gabriella frowned. "You know me so well. At the same time you hate me, don't you?"

"I don't hate you."

"Okay I'll play along. Why don't you?"

"Because I keep doing this, keep trying to separate myself from you and vice versa. But I never will be able to will I? Because you are me and I am..."

"You." Gabriella smiled.

They both looked at the house.

"Now do me a favor. Go get my niece."

The rain was relaxing as Tabitha was propped on the toilet, singing to herself. A lit cigarette sat on the edge of the sink, deepening the yellow burn mark in the white ceramic. She couldn't wait to see the look on Yvonna's face when she sent her to hell for killing her sister and nephews.

When she went to grab the cigarette and it dropped on the black and white tile floor, she picked it up, only to see Yvonna sitting on the edge of the tub.

She had been there the entire time. Hidden behind the shower curtain.

"What the fuck?" She jumped. Her body trembled and suddenly she felt a surge of diarrhea brewing. Already on the toilet, she was definitely in the right place at the wrong time.

"Where is she?" Yvonna asked calmly.

"Wow." Tabitha said shaking her head. "I guess...I guess...what they say is true."

"And what's that?"

"You're like the wind." She paused. "You feel it but you never know it's there."

"Where is my daughter?" Yvonna repeated.

"I don't know where—."

"Let me warn you, my patience is thin these days."

"But I don't—."

Yvonna threw her finger up. "And...I don't have time for lies. So I'm giving people who hate me little to no chance to fuck up. You're being warned."

"What are you going to do?"

"Well, if you don't give me an answer, I won't tie you up. I won't torture you. I won't even tell you your sister was a whore who slept with my nigga when she knew how much I loved him. And so she deserved to die." She smiled. "This is what will happen. If you don't give me the answer I'm looking for, I will kill you, nothing more, nothing less." She breathed deeply. "Now let me ask again, where is she? Where is my daughter? And where is Bilal?"

Splattered with dried blood, Yvonna sat in Jabar's car a mile down the road. She collected a few things from Tabitha's house, to get more clues on where her daughter was located. At the end of the day Tabitha provided little to no help. And for her lack of efforts, she was shot in the face.

Now with Tabitha's phone in hand, she scrolled through the many messages in her texting app. Messages from Bilal were inside too. She knew the cell held the information of where they detained her daughter; she just had to find it.

She also knew Delilah had been there, evident by the pink glitter ear buds she had in her lap. She was determined to find her, come hell or high water.

And just like Tabitha, anyone who got in her way would fall.

That was a promise.

She was still investigating Tabitha's phone when Gabe texted:

R U still shittin? Hurry the fuc up.

Yvonna texted:

Im comin. whats up tho

Nothin. We at Lydia's crib

She smiled and texted:

Shoot me the addy again

CHAPTER TWENTY-FOUR

It appeared that even the weather was up for a little revenge, because the rain resumed its power as thunder clapped the sky. Nature was alerting the world.

A storm was coming.

In the name of Yvonna Harris.

Holding court with his family, Gabe stood in the middle of the living room floor. He was at his girlfriend's townhome and Tahir and Oakes were with him. All were excited about the next day and sending a message through Bricks' people to get at Yvonna. The hope was that once she got the message, she would give herself up.

Things may have been going their way now, but earlier in the week Tahir fucked up on the low. Tahir drove by to see if Yvonna was at Bricks' Aunt Cora's. He was going to pass a letter demanding she offer up herself for her only child. Instead, using his friend's pink and black ice cream truck, he struck Chomps down.

After barely escaping with his life, when Bricks' family ran after it, since the expedition was solo, he was so embarrassed he didn't tell his siblings.

He almost messed up the mission.

Gabe had the phone pressed against his ear and when he didn't get an answer he hung up. "Fuck." He rubbed his temples and took a deep breath. "This...this ain't right."

Tahir dug into the popcorn bowl and popped a few in his mouth. Gabe's girl, Lydia Martina, had made the snacks for his family earlier and he was the only one who was in the mood to eat. "Why you so worried?" He shook some salt on the treat and ate from it again. "She said she's on the way."

"Like I said, something ain't right."

"If she don't show up today she'll come tomorrow. In time for the event. Tabitha not trying to miss this for nothing in the world."

Oakes sat back in the couch and sipped beer. "Yeah, you already gave her the address." He wiped his mouth with the back of his hand. "Chill out. You making me nervous as fuck."

"It ain't about being nervous." Gabe paced the floor and then flopped down on the sofa. "Nah, something else is wrong."

"The girl?" Tahir said, mouth full of food. "Where she at?"

"She's a spare."

They both smiled, getting the reference.

"Question, if the end game was to kill Yvonna, why bring her here?" Oakes asked, sipping the rest of his beer and opening another. "It seems dangerous."

"I was gonna say the same thing but I was having such a good time I decided to go with the flow." Tahir said.

"He doing it for money," Bilal said entering the room, hands tucked in his pockets. They didn't know he was there. "Ain't that right, unc? All of this, everything you doing is 'cause you trying to get paid?"

Gabe laughed. "Not your uncle remember?"

"Let me talk to him alone," Bilal said to the room.

Silence.

"Now." He said calmly.

The brothers looked at Gabe who nodded in approval. One by one they exited, Tahir with the bowl of popcorn in hand.

"You know, you're getting on my nerves." Gabe said. "My sibs wanted to get rid of you the moment you gave us the kid but I was like nah. He be something like family."

"So this all been about money?" Bilal continued, demanding an answer. He was tiring of being used. "You had me bring her here, just so you can —."

"What?" Gabe asked, flopping back on the sofa. "Finally get what this family deserves? A little restitution."

"But what about what she did to me?" Bilal slammed his fist over his chest. "I lost everybody behind this bitch! Everybody who gave a fuck about me. Getting paid won't solve my problems."

"Cry then, nigga."

"I'm not playing!" He roared.

He laughed at his might. "Just knowing she'll be taken care of should be good enough for you." Gabe said with a smile. "What does it matter if we make a come up? It's basically two birds with one stone."

"So you're auctioning her to the highest bidder aren't you?" Bilal continued. "That's it? Even if I thought it was best for me, I don't recall being offered a dime. Did you forget that part?"

"Okay, how much you want?"

Bilal took a deep breath. "When I was a baby, she lured my mother out of the house and I was taken by CPS. Then Yvonna posed me naked, took pictures and framed my mother to make it look like she was sexually abusing me. Even had her write a letter." He scratched his scalp in anger. "I can still remember the words."

"I don't want to hear no —."

"It said, 'To whomever reads this, I am so sorry for being less than a parent. I exposed my only son to a life that he never would've known otherwise. I never knew I had fantasies for him, until I met Caven. His love for boys heightened my sexual desires and made me realize that there's so much more to human sexuality. I know many people can't and won't understand this and because of it, I've chosen to take my own life and the life of my partner in this heinous crime. I only hope that you'll tell my son how much I loved him. With love, Sabrina.'"

Gabe hated to admit it but the letter was awful coming from a mother.

"But Yvonna wasn't done with me, nah," he said shaking his head. "After it all, then she placed lead paint chips in my soda, trying to kill me. They were able to save my life, but, but I never was the same. Always feeling like I was more outside my body than in, even now. So here I am, in the world, no mother, no Grams and now, no brothers. The only thing that keeps me going is waiting to see her drown in her own blood."

"Fuck is you telling me all this for?"

"Because if anybody deserves to kill her, if anybody deserves to see her drop, it's me. For me, it ain't about money. It never was."

"You wrong, young bull." Gabe sat back. "My sister gone. My nephews gone. And every nigga placing a bid to see her tortured and killed tomorrow lost someone by her hands. You ain't special. You just alone. Except for the fact that your father's death, her first one, started it all. Other than that, you just like me."

"Where is the girl?"

"Get out, young bull. I'm done talking."

CHAPTER TWENTY-FIVE

Oakes was lying on Lydia's basement floor knocked out. A smile wiped across his face when he felt a feminine hand nudging at his dick. He assumed he was dreaming and the last thing he wanted was to wake up before he came. And so, he continued to be pleased until his sperm oozed out. Once satisfied, with a smile on his face he opened his eyes just as Yvonna's hand slammed down over his mouth.

The dream became a nightmare.

She always was a nasty bitch.

When he tried to move, she pressed the knife against his neck. "I don't want to hurt you. But I will." She took a deep breath. "Where is she?"

He shook his head once.

"I won't ask again."

He shook his head once more and she sliced his neck. His flesh opened like butter under the blade and he felt blood drain from his body as his life washed away.

He was dying, all while looking up at her pretty face. She needed to be sure he would go to the after life, so she stayed over top of him, until his eyes shut and the blood dampened the carpet beneath.

Tahir was rolled over on his side, talking to something young and soft on the phone. His back was faced the door as he engaged heavily in conversation. He was at ease because the way he saw it, in a few days, he would have enough money to take his girl of the hour on vacation.

"Yeah, so he was licking my asshole right, while she was sucking my dick and — ."

"Are you lying, Tahir?" Brenda asked, getting moist at the idea of him being bisexual. "Because you know freaky shit turns me on. But not if you faking it."

"Does it matter if I'm lying if your pussy wet?" Tahir laughed softly.

"Good point."

"I can't wait to get into that shit too." When he heard the door open he said, "Hold on." He turned around. The light shined through from the hallway but he didn't see anyone. Figuring one of his brothers stepped inside and then left because he was busy, he turned back around and focused on the call.

"Who was it?" She asked.

"Nobody," he sighed deeply. "I thought it was one of my brothers at first. I be glad when this shit is over and we get that paper though."

"You keep saying that but you not telling me what the deal is. It's like you don't trust me or something. Where you getting this cash?"

"You twenty-four, I'm forty two," he chuckled. "Talk to me about trust when you get my age and…"

He felt the bed weigh down but when he turned his head to investigate this time, Yvonna was behind him, as if they were lovers. Except there was a blade to his throat. Her lips were against his ear. "Where is she?"

His eyes widened and his heart sped up. "I don't know." The phone dropped from his hand.

"I'll tell you like I told them, don't fuck with me." She nestled closer to him and pressed the blade deeper onto his neck. "Where is she? Where is Bilal?"

"I promise, I don't—."

"Hello." The girl on the phone said softly. "Tahir, you there?"

Silence.

"Tahir, answer me." She could hear a soft gurgling sound. "Are you okay?" Of course not. Because as she waited for him to return, Yvonna had softly slit his neck, snuffing out his life.

Yvonna tiptoed toward the master bedroom but when she walked inside she saw Gabe sitting on the windowsill. As if expecting her. "Where is Lydia?" He said. "She...she said she was going to the shower and...never came back."

She smiled. "You know where she is."

He took a deep breath. "Wow," he said softly. "The rumors are true."

"Let me guess...I'm like the wind." She paused. "You feel me but you never know I'm there."

Gabe smiled although inside his heart broke. Yvonna reciting the words meant one thing and one thing only, that his sister was also gone.

"The thing is, if people really believed that why do they continue to fuck with me?"

He looked down. "People coming here for you."

She smiled and took one step further inside. "No they aren't..."

He readjusted on the open windowsill and for a moment she thought back to her daughter, who on a night similar, took a leap just to be with Bilal.

"How you figure?" He asked.

She raised Tabitha's phone. "I redirected them. Including Hall." She placed it back into her pocket. "I've also flattened your car tires." She took a step closer. "So, Gabe, where is my daughter?"

He looked down at her hand and saw a knife dripping with blood. His body ran cold. "So...so you just gonna kill all of my people huh?" Suddenly having money meant nothing if he didn't have his siblings to share it with. "Ain't nothing sacred to you? You trying to take out my whole family!"

"Delilah," she said calmly. "Where is she?"

He looked at the knife again and then her frame. She was neither short nor tall, big or small. Just a woman. He took a deep breath. He would take his chances in the name of his family. So he stood up, but stayed next to the window. "Do you really think I can't hurt you? And get that knife out your hand?" He asked, preparing to charge her. "Do you really think you're stronger than a man? I—."

BOOM.

She let off one in his shoulder.

His eyes flew open.

He didn't see the gun.

He assumed since she was using the knife, she wasn't packing. But guns made too much noise and she liked to move quietly. Which is why she killed the others with a knife. But it didn't mean she wasn't ready for all scenarios.

She aimed higher as he held his arm. "Where is she?"

He smiled, turned around and jumped out the window.

"No! No! No!" When she rushed toward the window to see where he was she stumbled backwards.

He was gone.

Bilal sat on the back step smoking a cigarette. When he felt someone behind him, he didn't bother looking. He knew she was there. He heard the gunfire moments earlier. "It took you long enough."

She stepped closer and stood behind his turned back. "Where is my daughter, Bilal?"

"You ruin my life and that's all you got to say to me?"

She knew his wounds ran deep and he was the one person in her opinion who had a right to feel a certain way. And yet, she attempted to do right by him by hiring a lawyer to get him out of prison. For crimes he committed that had nothing to do with him. The plan was to do much more for him later in life, if ever he accepted her help.

"Bilal, I'm...I'm sorry, I really am. I did so much to you and I, I never stopped to think about how my actions would effect you."

"Not good enough."

"I understand."

"Kill him," Gabriella whispered. "What you waiting on? You let him live and he will take your life before the night is out. I promise."

"I don't care about what you understand." He flicked the cigarette across the way. "I care about getting what's mine."

"And what's that?"

"You know." He rose and stepped closer. "Your life."

They were face to face. Now that he was older, Yvonna's heart tripped several beats in his presence. He had her first love's entire face. The curly hair, the light skin, the Spanish and black heritage. And she both loved and hated him for the resemblance.

"Where is she, Bilal?"

"I don't know." He moved in.

"Guess."

"I said I don't know." He stepped closer.

"You brought her here and now her life is in danger." She continued whipping her gun out to halt his movements.

He stopped in his tracks.

"Now I'm sorry I messed up your life. I am, but there is nothing I won't do to save her. So for now, you coming with me."

CHAPTER TWENTY-SIX

Bilal was quiet as he piloted Jabar's car down the dark street, per Yvonna's request. But she kept the gun trained on him, in case he attempted to make a move. And it was obvious, from the look in his eyes that he wanted to hurt her badly.

"Be smart with him, Yvonna," Gabriella said from the backseat. "Be really smart."

"I don't know what that means."

"Think like him. Remember your younger years."

"Who you talking to?" He frowned, as he made a left. "Delilah be doing that shit too. Its weird as fuck."

"Are you sure you don't remember the address to Gabe's father's house? Or where Hall's girl lives?"

"I'm trying to remember." He shrugged. "But I can't right now. Maybe it's cause you're pointing a gun at me."

"He's lying," Gabriella said.

"Tell me about my father."

She frowned. Speaking about Bilal Sr. wasn't going to help her current situation. "What you wanna know?"

"Anything..." he shrugged. "I mean, was he a preacher type or—."

"Nowhere near a preacher."

"Well tell me something." He continued. "I mean, I was too young to remember the stories from when my grandmother was alive. Then you killed her."

She looked away. To be honest she was tiring of the pity party. Everybody lost somebody at one time or another. "Stop it, Bilal."

"Stop what?!" He yelled. "You did kill my grandmother. And the world knows." He continued to drive. "The least you can do is be honest about it."

"I said I'm sorry. That doesn't mean you can have my daughter."

"Does that help you sleep at night? Because it doesn't do shit for me."

She sighed deeply. "Keep your eyes focused for his father's car."

"I said okay."

She looked away and back at him. "He was very strong but sweet too. Sometimes." She giggled a little. "I think because he was light skin, he thought people would disrespect but they never did. They used to call him a Ruthless Mothafucka with manners."

He chuckled.

"I'm serious," she smiled. "He would rip your heart out but at the same time, he cared about those he held close. He didn't do violence for the sake of violence. With him, there always had to be a reason."

"So if he was so great, why kill him?"

"He was also a whore."

He glared.

"And I killed him because you were born. And you shouldn't have been born." She shook her head. "Your mother was one of my friends and she slept with my man behind my back. I mean, you're young, Bilal. And I was too. When you're young you make mistakes. I mean, ain't nobody ever love you enough to kill for you?"

"Nah. Not yet."

"Well she's out there." She looked out the window. "Trust me."

He sighed. "My dad had a tattoo on him that read, 'LALVON'. What was that about? Don't nobody know."

"It means Bilal and Yvonna to the end. The Lal is the end of his name, the Von is the middle of mine."

"So he fucked with you like that? To put ink on his body?"

"I told you we were real. It wasn't a game." She readjusted and lowered the weapon a little. "Bilal, where is the car? And where is Delilah? "

"I told you, I really don't know." He shrugged. "I wish I did but I don't. I would've told you long ago so this shit could be over and I could get on with my life."

She didn't believe him but she knew he was holding his ground. "Pull over. Up the street."

"Why?"

"Pull over." She said a bit louder, raising the gun.

He complied.

"Get out," she continued.

"So you 'spect me to believe you just gonna let me go? Even though you don't have Delilah?"

"If you don't know where she is, I can't push anymore. I have to trust that you're telling the truth and look some place else. Now get out."

"Why won't you kill me?"

"Because you're the one person on earth I can't kill. Now leave. Before I'm forced to change my mind."

He pulled the car door open. "I won't stop looking for you."

"I know." She said honestly. "And I'll be waiting. I'll always be waiting."

Bilal and Delilah walked toward the motel room he stayed in from time to time in Hyattsville, Maryland. It was a low-key establishment littered with youth, mainly because the government paid for young men under the age of twenty-five to take residence there if they could prove they were looking for gainful employment.

Of course he wasn't seeking a job.

He was seeking Yvonna's head.

But that didn't mean he wasn't fine enough to get a few women to lie for his benefit. And that's exactly what happened.

After Yvonna dropped him off on a road, and he realized the coast was clear, he sat on a stranger's front porch and thought about what Gabe said to his siblings when asked where Delilah was.

The term he remembered Gabe using was, *she's a spare.*

After some creative thinking on his part, he realized that a spare often referred to an extra tire in the trunk of a car and so he went to the detached garage in the back of Gabe's girlfriend's house. And parked inside, was an old 1976 Volvo that could do nothing but stare at spectators because the engine was snatched long ago.

After popping the trunk and walking around the back, there inside he saw Delilah, gagged and crying. After freeing her, he caught an Uber to the motel. Although killing Yvonna was still on his mind, for the moment, all he wanted was to go inside the room and get some sleep. He figured once rested, he could come up with another plan.

The only thing he was sure of at the moment was that he was in love with Delilah. And wanted to keep her safe from his surrogate family, despite her mother's evil ways. She was the daughter of the woman who killed everyone he loved. And he loved her; it was the most difficult thing he ever had to admit.

For starters, every time he saw her, he saw a glimpse of Yvonna. That beautiful, evil, alluring, scary face. Secondly, she was the only one who understood what he was going through. Her mother was a serial killer. His father was her victim and so that meant they lived in infamy.

When the door opened, both almost choked when they saw Yvonna sitting on the bed. "Don't run." Yvonna said, pointing the gun at Bilal. "I'm not going anywhere."

"Mom!" Delilah said, covering her mouth with a quivering hand. "What...what you doing here?"

She rose. "Come in." She snatched Delilah by the arm.

Bilal followed and closed the door. He hung next to it, hands in his pockets, rocking.

Delilah approached Yvonna. "Mom, how did you...how did you know?"

"I read your messages." Her eyes remained on Bilal. "On your laptop."

"Why you ain't come here first then?" Bilal asked. "If you knew we were here and shit?"

He was a disrespectful ass nigga. "Because I needed to kill everybody who saw her face."

"Kill everybody?" Delilah repeated. "Mom...what's going on with you? Is it true what Bilal was saying?"

"Depends on what he told you."

"Mom!"

"It's time to leave."

"I'm not...I'm not going back with you. I love it here."

"You don't have a choice, Delilah. There are people who want me dead and you have my face. That means they'll never let you live in peace. Don't you get it? Ever!"

"But I love him!" She stood next to Bilal.

"And I love her." He grinned sinisterly.

"You also want me dead." She shrugged. "So tell me, what kind of love can be built off hate?"

"You tell me." He shrugged. "You claimed to hate and love my father. And he gone."

"Anyway, he doesn't want you dead, mom." Delilah said.

"Ask him." Yvonna said pointing the gun in his direction.

Delilah looked at him. "You don't...you don't wanna kill my mother do you?"

Silence.

"Bilal." Delilah whispered.

"You want the truth or a lie? Cause I don't wanna start our life together lying. At the end of the day it's like this, you either wanna be with me, or you want to go back with her. You gotta choose. Right here. Right now."

Yvonna grabbed Delilah's hand and walked toward the door where Bilal stood. She was making the decision for her. "I told you. We have to..." Suddenly a searing pain ripped through her belly. When she looked down Bilal was holding a bloody knife.

He smiled. "I knew you were reading her messages. And I knew you would come."

The gun dropped and Yvonna fell to the floor, hands on the bleeding wound.

"Bilal, please...please don't," Delilah begged, body shivering.

He placed the gun in the back of his pants and lowered his height. Once down, he stabbed Yvonna again in the stomach. Then he looked up at Delilah and aimed the blade toward her, before flipping it so that the handle was in her direction. "If you want me, our lives start right here. Because you have to understand, as long as she's alive, she will never let us be."

"Bilal, no," she said softly, tears rolling down her face.

"Come here, bae," he extended his hand upward. "Come."

She took his hand and dropped to her knees, on the other side of Yvonna's body.

"Please don't do this," Yvonna begged looking at her only child. "Please don't...don't do this to yourself."

"She just thinking about herself," he said.

She grabbed her hand. "Listen to me, you don't wanna do this," she said as tears strolled back. "If he wants to kill me, let him do it his self, but you won't be able to have this on your heart. I promise. The guilt will be too much."

He held out the weapon. "Do it, Delilah. If you love me."

"Give me the knife, I'll do it myself," Yvonna pleaded.

In that moment it was obvious how much she cared. She was willing to take her own life, so Delilah wouldn't live with grief. But Bilal didn't want to just see her die, he wanted her in pain, like he was all his life.

And what better way to do this, than to get her daughter to assist in her murder?

"No...I want her to do it." He looked at his girl. "Give me your hand."

Delilah removed her grasp from her mother and took the weapon soaked in her blood instead. Wiping

snot and tears from her face she asked, "Are you sure you want me, Bilal?"

"More than anything," he said, reaching over Yvonna's body, to kiss her slimy, snotty lips.

"Do you promise to never leave me?"

"I will never fucking leave you. You hear me? Ever."

With that she looked into his eyes, and plunged the knife into her mother's stomach. Yvonna blurted a bubble of air and slowly closed her eyes.

Stunned at her own actions, she dropped the knife. Rising slowly, she looked down at her bloody body. "Oh my God...I...I...just stabbed her. I just stabbed mommy."

Bilal rose and held her closely. Placing his hands on both sides of her face he said, "Hey, hey, it's okay."

"I killed my mother!"

"*We* killed her, and its okay." He said gripping her arms. "You hear me? She had this shit coming. She had it coming."

Delilah was beyond consoling and continued to cry profusely. "I'm so afraid. I'm so...fucking..."

"Let's go," he said yanking her hand, as he went around the room, tucking money and important items into his pockets.

When they made it outside, he activated the alarm to a car he never used but had on the ready. Because he knew Yvonna was coming, he planned everything, including fresh clothes and cash. His only problem was he didn't have the rush of adrenaline he thought he would when he avenged his family's death.

But why?

Maybe it was because he was somewhat disappointed that she died so easily. That she died for love. He heard about her being the un-killable one and now he realized all was a lie. She died as easily as the rest.

As he drove down the street, he looked over at Delilah and grabbed her hand. "You got me in your life. You hear me? You got me and that's all you should care about."

"You promise?"

"It's me and you forever," he said. "And we should get some tats too."

"That say what?" She sniffled.

He thought about what Yvonna said and smiled. After all, he had a girl who would kill for him too. Shouldn't it be official? "It should say *LalLah Land*."

"What's...what's that?"

"It means Bilal and Delilah forever."

She smiled. "So what can we do? I mean, what we gonna do to get money?"

"I'll think of everything. Trust me, you won't go without. Not a day." When his phone rang he answered. "Yeah?"

"You gotta get ghost, Yvonna is onto us," Gabe said anxiously.

"Where are you?"

"Getting a bullet wound stitched at a friend's house. She fucking shot me! That bitch shot me! And she killed everybody, man. Everybody but me and Hall gone!"

"Tabitha too?"

"Yes."

Bilal smiled. Yvonna wasn't worthless after all. Because if she hadn't dropped by Yvonna's hand, he had plans to do it himself. "Yeah, well you won't have to worry 'bout her no more."

"What that mean?"

He looked at Delilah whose head was leaning against the window. She looked dazed and in pain.

"Like I said, she gone. Me and my shawty saw to that shit."

"Gone as in dead?"

He glared. "Is there any other kind of dead?"

Delilah wept louder.

"Are you sure?" Gabe asked.

For some reason, the words rocked harder than he expected. If he said she was dead, why didn't he believe him? "Yeah I'm sure. Fuck you keep asking for?"

He chuckled. "Okay, nigga. I hear you but I'll say this...she has come back from the dead before. And if you didn't kill her, you'll wish you did if she's alive. I know that much."

He shifted a little. Almost hitting a car when he yanked the steering wheel too hard. "Well she won't be coming back this time."

A few drivers beeped at him.

He beeped back.

"Unless you saw her turn blue, I don't trust it. Good luck sleeping tonight." He hung up.

Two hours later, when Delilah was asleep in their new motel room, Bilal left. He had to go back to the motel. Once there, he didn't even get out the car. He just watched to see if she came out. He knew showing back up to the scene of a murder was dangerous but Gabe made him feel a kind of way.

Was he right?

Did Yvonna escape death?

Again?

He needed to slice her throat, just to be sure.

When he couldn't take wondering anymore, he exited the car and moved down the walkway. When he made it to the door, he looked left and using his key card, entered. His heart dropped when he saw the bloodstain on the floor.

And Yvonna Harris gone.

EPILOGUE

Bricks sat on the bed as Jabar made repeated calls to Yvonna's phone. He looked concerned and his anxiousness bothered Bricks. "What's wrong?"

"Shut up!" Jabar yelled aiming the gun in his direction. "I'm sick of hearing your fucking mouth."

"Look, is something wrong with my wife or not, nigga?"

He put the cell phone down. "Nah, I mean, it's getting late and she told me she would call by now. Just wondering what's taking so long."

"Maybe we should go out looking for her."

"*We* not going to do shit." He picked up the phone and dialed again. "If something's wrong I'll go looking and you'll be dead."

CLACK.

Jabar jumped when he heard something tossed at the window. "Fuck is that?"

CLACK. CLACK. CLACK.

Jabar walked backwards, still aiming the gun in Bricks' direction as he moved to the window. "I know these lil niggas not throwing rocks at the—." When he pushed the yellow curtain back, he saw Raul with a handful of rocks and ten grown men behind him with guns.

Next he heard a firm knock at the door.

Bricks smiled.

He was right after all when he told Amanda his family would follow. And although he didn't see any of them trailing him when he left Aunt Cora's house, he knew they were always watching.

"Remember those many lives I told you I had? Well I'ma use one now." He laughed softly. "And if I were you I'd open the door. Unless you in the mood to die."

EARLIER THAT NIGHT

After Bilal and Delilah crept away from his motel room, Zamia and Aunt Cora, along with three of her nephews, sat tucked in the parking lot in an old pick up truck. Just like they had spread out and been following Bricks, they had also made sure to tail Yvonna. After all, it was best to keep eyes on your enemies at all times.

So when Bilal and Delilah exited the room, they figured it was time to see what was going on. Because they saw Yvonna go inside.

So where was she now?

"It's time." Aunt Cora pushed the door open.

They piled out of the truck, and Zamia, a career door picker, popped the flimsy motel lock leading to the room. There on the floor was Yvonna soaking in her own blood.

"Oh, snap, auntie, they killed her." Zamia said covering her mouth with trembling fingers. "I wanted to be the one to dead her ass."

"You still can." Aunt Cora noticed Yvonna's short shallow breaths. "Cause this bitch ain't dead," she turned back and looked at her nephews. "Scoop her up boys and throw her in the hatch. I guess its left up to us to take out the trash."

COMING SOON

BILAL & DELILAH
A SHYT LIST NOVEL

CARTEL PUBLICATIONS

PRESENTS

The Cartel Publications Order Form

www.thecartelpublications.com

Inmates **ONLY** receive novels for $10.00 per book **PLUS** shipping fee **PER BOOK.**

(Mail Order **MUST** come from inmate directly to receive discount)

Shyt List 1	_____	$15.00
Shyt List 2	_____	$15.00
Shyt List 3	_____	$15.00
Shyt List 4	_____	$15.00
Shyt List 5	_____	$15.00
Shyt List 6	_____	$15.00
Pitbulls In A Skirt	_____	$15.00
Pitbulls In A Skirt 2	_____	$15.00
Pitbulls In A Skirt 3	_____	$15.00
Pitbulls In A Skirt 4	_____	$15.00
Pitbulls In A Skirt 5	_____	$15.00
Victoria's Secret	_____	$15.00
Poison 1	_____	$15.00
Poison 2	_____	$15.00
Hell Razor Honeys	_____	$15.00
Hell Razor Honeys 2	_____	$15.00
A Hustler's Son	_____	$15.00
A Hustler's Son 2	_____	$15.00
Black and Ugly	_____	$15.00
Black and Ugly As Ever	_____	$15.00
Ms Wayne & The Queens of DC **(LGBT)**	_____	$15.00
Black And The Ugliest	_____	$15.00
Year Of The Crackmom	_____	$15.00
Deadheads	_____	$15.00
The Face That Launched A Thousand Bullets	_____	$15.00
The Unusual Suspects	_____	$15.00
Paid In Blood	_____	$15.00
Raunchy	_____	$15.00
Raunchy 2	_____	$15.00
Raunchy 3	_____	$15.00
Mad Maxxx (4th Book Raunchy Series)	_____	$15.00
Quita's Dayscare Center	_____	$15.00
Quita's Dayscare Center 2	_____	$15.00
Pretty Kings	_____	$15.00
Pretty Kings 2	_____	$15.00
Pretty Kings 3	_____	$15.00
Pretty Kings 4	_____	$15.00
Silence Of The Nine	_____	$15.00
Silence Of The Nine 2	_____	$15.00
Silence Of The Nine 3	_____	$15.00
Prison Throne	_____	$15.00

By Reign

Drunk & Hot Girls _____ $15.00
Hersband Material **(LGBT)** _____ $15.00
The End: How To Write A _____ $15.00
Bestselling Novel In 30 Days (Non-Fiction Guide)
Upscale Kittens _____ $15.00
Wake & Bake Boys _____ $15.00
Young & Dumb _____ $15.00
Young & Dumb 2: Vyce's Getback _____ $15.00
Tranny 911 **(LGBT)** _____ $15.00
Tranny 911: Dixie's Rise **(LGBT)** _____ $15.00
First Comes Love, Then Comes Murder _____ $15.00
Luxury Tax _____ $15.00
The Lying King _____ $15.00
Crazy Kind Of Love _____ $15.00
Goon _____ $15.00
And They Call Me God _____ $15.00
The Ungrateful Bastards _____ $15.00
Lipstick Dom **(LGBT)** _____ $15.00
A School of Dolls **(LGBT)** _____ $15.00
Hoetic Justice _____ $15.00
KALI: Raunchy Relived _____ $15.00
(5th Book in Raunchy Series)
Skeezers _____ $15.00
Skeezers 2 _____ $15.00
You Kissed Me, Now I Own You _____ $15.00
Nefarious _____ $15.00
Redbone 3: The Rise of The Fold _____ $15.00
The Fold (4th Redbone Book) _____ $15.00
Clown Niggas _____ $15.00
The One You Shouldn't Trust _____ $15.00
The WHORE The Wind
Blew My Way _____ $15.00
She Brings The Worst Kind _____ $15.00
The House That Crack Built _____ $15.00
The House That Crack Built 2 _____ $15.00
The House That Crack Built 3 _____ $15.00
The House That Crack Built 4 _____ $15.00
Level Up **(LGBT)** _____ $15.00
Villains: It's Savage Season _____ $15.00
Gay For My Bae _____ $15.00
War _____ $15.00
War 2: All Hell Breaks Loose _____ $15.00
War 3: The Land Of The Lou's _____ $15.00
War 4: Skull Island _____ $15.00

(Redbone 1 & 2 are **NOT** Cartel Publications novels and if **ordered** the cost is **FULL** price of $15.00 **each. No Exceptions**.)

Please add **$5.00** for shipping and handling fees for up to **(2) BOOKS PER ORDER**.

Inmates too!

(See Next Page for ORDER DETAILS)

<u>The Cartel Publications * P.O. BOX 486 OWINGS MILLS MD 21117</u>

Name: _____

Address: _____

City/State: _____

Contact/Email: _____

*Please allow 8-10 <u>**BUSINESS**</u> days <u>**Before**</u> shipping.*

*The Cartel Publications is <u>**NOT**</u> responsible for <u>**Prison Orders**</u> rejected!*

<u>NO RETURNS and NO REFUNDS</u>
<u>NO PERSONAL CHECKS ACCEPTED</u>
<u>STAMPS NO LONGER ACCEPTED</u>

Made in the USA
Monee, IL
26 August 2021